B.J. Daniels is a *New York Times* and *USA TODAY* bestselling author. She wrote her first book after a career as an award-winning newspaper journalist and author of thirty-seven published short stories. She lives in Montana with her husband, Parker, and three springer spaniels. When not writing, she quilts, boats and plays tennis. Contact her at bjdaniels.com, on Facebook or on Twitter, @bjdanielsauthor.

Rogue Gunslinger

B.J. DANIELS

MILLS & BOON

First published in Great Britain 2018
by Mills & Boon, an imprint of HarperCollins*Publishers*
1 London Bridge Street, London, SE1 9GF

Large Print edition 2018

ISBN: 978-0-263-08318-7

MIX
Paper from
responsible sources
FSC
www.fsc.org   FSC™ C007454

This book is produced from independently certified FSC™ paper to ensure responsible forest management. For more information visit www.harpercollins.co.uk/green.

Printed and bound in Great Britain
by CPI Group (UK) Ltd, Croydon, CR0 4YY

This book is for Gale Simonson,
part of the Simonson duo,
who keeps our lives interesting in the
Quilting by the Border group. You
are always like a breath of fresh air.
Thanks for keeping me smiling.

Chapter One

The old antique Royal typewriter clacked with each angry stroke of the keys. Shaking fingers pounded out livid words onto the old discolored paper. As the fury built, the fingers moved faster and faster until the keys all tangled together in a metal knot that lay suspended over the paper.

With a curse of frustration, the metal arms were tugged apart and the sound of the typewriter resumed in the small room. Angry words burst across the page, some letters darker than others as the keystrokes hit like a hammer. Other letters appeared lighter, some dropping down a half line as the fingers slipped from the worn keys. A bell sounded at the end of each line as the carriage was returned with a clang, until the paper was ripped from the typewriter.

Read in a cold, dark rage, the paper was folded hurriedly, the edges uneven, and stuffed into the envelope already addressed in the black typewritten letters:

Author TJ St. Clair
Whitehorse, Montana

The stamp slapped on, the envelope sealed, the fingers still shaking with expectation for when the novelist opened it. The fan rose and smiled. Wouldn't Ms. St. Clair, aka Tessa Jane Clementine, love this one.

TJ St. Clair hated conference calls. Especially this conference call.

"I know it's tough with your book coming

out before Christmas," said Rachel, the marketing coordinator, the woman's voice sounding hollow on speakerphone in TJ's small New York City apartment.

"But I don't have to tell you how important it is to do as much promo as you can this week to get those sales where you want them," Sherry from Publicity and Events added.

TJ held her head and said nothing for a moment. "I'm going home for the holidays to be with my sisters, who I haven't seen in months." She started to say she knew how important promoting her book was, but in truth she often questioned if a lot of the events really made that much difference—let alone all the social media. If readers spent as much time as TJ had to on social media, she questioned how they could have time to read books.

"It's the threatening letters you've been getting, isn't it?" her agent Clara said.

She glanced toward the window, hating to

admit that the letters had more than spooked her. "That is definitely part of it. They have been getting more…detailed and more threatening."

"I'm so sorry, TJ," Clara said and everyone added in words of sympathy.

"You've spoken to the police?" her editor, Dan French, asked.

"There is nothing they can do until…until the fan acts on the threats. That's another reason I want to go to Montana."

For a few beats there was silence. "All right. I can speak to Marketing," Dan said. "We'll do what we can from this end."

"I hate to request this, but is there any chance you could do a couple of book signings while you're at home before Christmas, right before the book comes out?" Rachel asked. "I wouldn't push, but TJ, we hate to see you lose the momentum you've picked up with your last book."

"That would be at least something," Dan agreed.

"If you don't make the list, it won't be the end of the world," her editor added. "But we'd hoped to see you advance up the list with this one. I love this book. I think it's the best one you've ever written."

The first week a book came out was the most important and they all knew it. If she didn't make the list—the *New York Times* list— it would mean losing the bonus she usually got for ranking in the top ten. It would also hurt her on her next contract, not to mention the publisher might back off on promotional money for her.

"We don't mean to pressure you," Dan said. "But I'm sure if the police thought this fan was really dangerous—"

"I think going to Montana is smart," her agent cut in. "You'll be safe there with your family over the holidays. We can regroup when you get back."

She rubbed her temples. "I could do one book signing in my hometown since there is only one bookstore there. Whitehorse is tiny and in the middle of nowhere. The roads can be closed off and on this time of year, so there won't be much of a turnout though."

"Isn't the *Billings Gazette* doing a story on you as well?" Trish from Marketing asked.

"Yes." She groaned inwardly, having forgotten she'd agreed to that months ago.

"That will have to do, then," her agent said, coming to her defense. "Her next book will be out in the spring. Let's plan on doing something special for that."

"We have ads coming out in six major magazines as well as a social media blitz for this one," Rachel said. "You should be fine. You have a lot of loyal fans who've been waiting patiently for this book. Your presales are good."

"Are you all right with this?" her agent asked.

She nodded and then realized she had to speak. Her throat was dry, her stomach roiling. Just the thought of any kind of public event had her terrified. But before she could answer, the call was over. Everyone wished each other a happy and safe holiday and hung up, except for her agent.

"Are you sure you're okay?"

"I will be once I get home," she told her and herself. She couldn't wait to get on the plane. She hadn't been back to Montana for years except for her grandmother's funeral.

"Keep in touch. And if you need anything…"

TJ smiled. She loved her agent. "I know. Thank you." She disconnected. Every book release she worried it wouldn't make the list or wouldn't be high enough on the list—which meant better than the last book had done. Not this time.

"You have bigger things to worry about at the moment," she said to herself as she walked to her apartment window and looked out.

I know where you live. You think you can sit in your big-city apartment and ignore me? Think again.

That ominous threat was added at the bottom of the last written attack she'd received from True Fan. What was different this time was that her fan had included a photograph taken from the outside of her New York City apartment. She'd recognized the curtains covering the window of her third-floor unit. There'd been a light behind them, which meant she'd been home when her "fan" had taken the photo from the sidewalk outside.

It was recent too. One of the wings of Mrs. Gunderson's Christmas angel was in the photograph. Her elderly neighbor had put it up only two days ago. TJ had helped her.

Just the thought of how recent the photo had been taken made her shudder. She glanced at her phone. Her flight was still hours away but she preferred sitting at the airport surrounded by security screened people to staying another minute in this apartment.

Sticking her phone into a side pocket of her purse, she grabbed the handle of her suitcase and headed for the door.

Nowadays she always checked the hallway before she left her apartment. She did this time as well. It was empty. She could hear holiday music playing in one of the apartments down the hall. The song brought tears to her eyes. She was a mess, way too emotional to spend the holidays with her sisters—especially since the three of them had been estranged for months.

She hesitated. Maybe she should change her

flight. Go to some warm resort. But just the thought turned her stomach. She was going back to Whitehorse. Going home for Christmas.

She rolled her suitcase down to the elevator and pushed the button.

When it clanged its way up from what sounded like the basement, she waited for the door to open. If anyone she didn't recognize happened to be on the elevator, she would make an excuse about forgetting something she needed in her apartment and turn back until the elevator left again.

She knew it was silly, but she couldn't help it. No one was taking the threats seriously. But she had watched the tone of the letters degenerate into angry, hateful words that were more than threatening. This person wasn't done with her. Far from it. She couldn't shake the feeling that her "True Fan" was coming for her.

The elevator stopped and the door began to

open. Empty. She let out the breath she'd been holding. Stepping in, she pulled her suitcase close and pushed the button for the ground floor.

The fan writing her the threatening letters could be anyone. That was what was so frightening. It could even be someone who lived in this apartment complex. Or someone she'd met at a conference. She met so many fans, she couldn't possibly remember them all. It embarrassed her when they complimented her books. She wanted to hug them all. She doubted she would ever get used to this. Writing had been her dream since she was a girl. Getting published? Well, that was like a miracle to her. She couldn't believe her good luck.

Until she'd begun getting the letters from her True Fan.

Outside the apartment building, the sidewalk was filled with people hurrying past. Shoppers laden with packages, others rushing off to work… The city was bustling more than usual. She glanced at the faces of people as they passed, not sure what she was looking for. Would she recognize her rabid fan if she saw him or her?

She couldn't help studying their faces, looking for one that might be familiar. She didn't even know if her "fan" was male or female. She also didn't know if the person was watching her right now.

After a while, everyone began to look familiar to her. If anyone made eye contact, she quickly dropped her gaze as she made her way to the curb to signal for a cab. She wrote about crazed homicidal people. Wouldn't she recognize something in True Fan's eyes that would give the person away?

With a screech of brakes, a yellow cab came to a stop on the other side of the street. The driver motioned for her to hurry. But a large delivery truck was coming too fast for her to cross before it passed.

She felt something hit her in the back. Letting out a cry, she found herself falling into the street in front of the large speeding truck.

Chapter Two

It happened so fast. One minute she was standing on the curb waiting for the large delivery truck to pass before crossing the street to the waiting taxi.

The next she was falling forward into the street and the truck bearing down on her. Her arms windmilled as she tried to catch herself, but there was nothing to grab. She could hear the deafening roar of the truck's engine, smelled diesel fuel turning the air gray and closed her eyes as she realized she was about to die.

The hand that closed over her arm was large

and viselike. One minute she was falling head-long into the street in front of the truck and the next she was snatched from the crushing metal bumper as the truck roared on past.

Pulled by the hand gripping her arm, her body whipped back. She slammed into something so solid it could have been a lamppost. She turned just quickly enough that her face came in contact with the chest of a large male body as she tried to get her feet under her. He steadied her for a moment before the fingers on her arm released.

She looked up in time to see the man who'd saved her turn and walk away as if rescuing women was something he did every day. Trembling all over, she was still reeling from her near death.

"Wait!" she called after him. He'd just saved her life. But if he'd heard her, he didn't turn. All she got was a brief glimpse of granite features, collar-length dark, curly hair beneath a baseball cap above wide shoulders clad in a tan suede sheepskin coat before he disappeared into the crowd.

She turned to find her suitcase and purse had fallen to the ground at the edge of the curb. Still shaken, she reached for them. The taxi that had stopped for her was long gone. No one seemed to have noticed what had almost happened to her.

Why had the man taken off the way he had? A Good Samaritan who didn't like taking credit for his deeds? Or, she thought with a shudder, the person who'd pushed her in front of the speeding truck—and then saved her.

Was it possible the man had been her True Fan?

She remembered being hit from behind and then the viselike grip of his large hand as his fingers bit into her arm. He hadn't even taken the time to see if she was all right. A shudder rattled through her. Had this been a warning?

A cab pulled to a stop in front of her. Tears burned her eyes as she stepped toward it. After all this time of being away, she couldn't wait to go home to Whitehorse.

SILAS WALKER SWORE. He'd lost the man he'd been following in the crowd of Christmas shoppers. Now he leaned against the front of a building, watching the street. His leg hurt like hell. He realized he was limping badly and cursed. If it wasn't for his injury, he wouldn't have lost the man.

Or if he hadn't stopped just long enough to grab that woman who'd been jostled by the crowd and almost fallen in front of a delivery truck. He shook his head. She should have known better than to stand that close to the street, especially with the sidewalk this crowded. He hated to think what could have happened if he hadn't been right behind her.

His cell phone vibrated. He checked the

screen. A text from his boss that he wanted to see him ASAP. That couldn't be good. He quickly texted back that he was on his way.

One look at the way he was limping and he knew exactly what his boss was going to say. He'd come back to work too soon. That he knew his boss was right didn't make it any easier to accept.

But after today, after messing up an easy tail, Silas had to accept that he wasn't up to the job yet. That alone would force him to lay off his leg for a while. Just over the holidays, not that he was happy about it.

A taxi pulled past. He spotted the woman in the back seat. She wore a bright red long coat with a multicolored scarf—the same woman he'd grabbed out of the way of the truck.

But that wasn't the surprising part. He recognized her. He'd studied that face on the back cover of her book more times than he wanted to admit. He couldn't believe his luck. TJ St.

Clair. The thriller writer. Her photo hadn't done her justice.

As the taxi drove on past, he realized she was probably headed for the airport given that he now recalled seeing a suitcase next to her. Somewhere for the holidays?

Smiling, he told himself she might be headed home to Montana. If he was right… Well, what were the chances they might cross paths again?

TJ HAD WONDERED what it would be like seeing her sisters again. The last time they'd been together they'd argued. Well, that is, she and Chloe had argued with their younger sister Annabelle over their grandmother's house.

Grandmother Frannie Clementine had died a few months ago. In her will, she'd left everything she had—basically her house in Whitehorse—to Annabelle.

"Did you know she was going to do that?" they'd demanded.

"No, I swear I didn't," Annabelle had said on the phone since she hadn't attended the funeral or seen the will.

"Why would she do that?" Chloe had demanded.

"I have no idea," their sister had said. "Except...well, I always got the impression that she liked me the best." She'd tried to pass that off as a joke, but they'd all hung up angry.

Now as TJ stepped off the plane, she felt bad about the argument. The house had turned out to be a whole lot of work—and had held some surprises that neither TJ nor Chloe would have wanted to handle. It had been clear why Grandma Frannie had left the house to Annabelle, who they all agreed was more like Frannie than either TJ or Chloe.

The Billings, Montana, airport was small by most airport standards and sat on rimrocks overlooking the state's largest city. She hadn't gone far when she saw her sisters waving at her from the bottom of the escalator.

TJ couldn't help but grin. They were both wearing elf hats. She groaned. "This has to have been Annabelle's idea," she said under her breath. But the sight of them in those hats had definitely broken the ice.

She laughed as she reached them, hugging one and then the other. As she pulled back, she felt such a surge of love for her sisters that it brought tears to her eyes.

"We didn't want you to feel left out," Annabelle said, and whipped an elf hat from her bag and settled it on TJ's blonde head. She grinned and put her arm around them. "We look like triplets."

"Heaven forbid," Chloe said.

"I'm starving," Annabelle said, surprising no one. Since she'd quit modeling for a living, she was always hungry. "Ray J's barbecue when we get home, eat here or just get snacks like we used to for the ride home?"

"Snacks!" TJ and Chloe said together.

"Did I mention I bought your favorite bottles of wine?" Annabelle asked. "Or we can go out and party tonight."

TJ and Chloe groaned in unison and then laughed. It felt good being around them again, TJ thought, and felt her eyes burn again with tears. Coming home for the holidays had been the right choice. She realized this was the best she'd felt in a very long time.

Annabelle chattered as they walked through the terminal toward the exit. TJ half listened, thankful that the trouble between them had blown over. They were all three back in Montana just like when they were growing up. They were sisters and she couldn't have been more delighted to be with them, even though people stared.

She laughed. She'd forgotten they were all

now wearing elf hats. For a few minutes, she'd completely forgotten her near-death experience this morning in the city and True Fan's threats.

But as she and her sisters passed a group waiting in one of the departure lines, she saw a woman raise her phone and take a photo of the three of them. Glancing back, TJ saw the woman quickly begin texting someone.

Chapter Three

"Wow," Chloe cried from the front seat of the SUV as she showed TJ her phone. "It's already all over social media." There was the photograph of the three of them in their elf hats. Just as she'd feared, the woman had recognized her, tagging the photo with her pen name. "Ah the life of the rich and famous."

TJ groaned. "Now everyone will know that I've come home to Whitehorse for Christmas."

"It isn't like it was a secret, right?" Annabelle asked as she drove. "Everyone knows you're from Whitehorse, Montana. Not much of a leap that you would be going home for

Christmas." She glanced in the rearview mirror. "Seriously, is it a problem?"

"No," TJ lied. "It's fine. Sometimes it would be nice to be anonymous though, but I don't have to tell you about that."

Annabelle sighed. "Yep, but when now faced with being anonymous the rest of my life... Well, it's an adjustment. I have to admit, it was fun seeing my photo on the front of magazines—even if it was a doctored photo of me. Nothing is all that real with modeling."

"So you're not going back to it?" Chloe asked their baby sister. "You're just going to marry Dawson Rogers, become a ranchwoman—"

"And live happily ever after," Annabelle said with a giggle. "Yep, that's the plan."

They began discussing people they knew in Whitehorse and how things had or hadn't changed.

TJ only half listened to their conversation. She hadn't told either sister about the threat-

ening letters—let alone what had happened
in the city only hours ago. The more she'd
thought about it on the plane ride back to Montana, the more unsure she was that she'd been
pushed in front of that truck. Could it have
been an accident? Or had it been deliberate?
Either way, if that man hadn't grabbed her…

She shivered and looked out at the snowy
landscape. If that man was her True Fan, he'd
been watching her apartment. When the light
had gone off in her living room, he would have
known she would be coming downstairs. Or
he might have been a stranger passing by.

TJ shook her head, determined not to think
about it. She was safe now. At least for a while.

"So we're talking wedding bells," Chloe was
saying.

"Wait, I must have missed something," TJ
said, sitting forward to hear. "You and Dawson? When?"

"We haven't set a date yet. I know it's quick,

but I would love a Christmas wedding, something small and intimate," Annabelle said, sounding dreamy. Both Chloe and TJ groaned and then laughed.

"Love," Chloe said with a shake of her head.

"Actually," TJ said, settling back into her seat, "I always thought you and Dawson were a good match."

They talked about weddings, growing up in Whitehorse, people they knew who'd left— and those who had stayed. The time passed quickly on the drive to their hometown.

As they pulled up in front of the house they'd grown up in after their parents had died, Annabelle cut the engine. Conversation died. They all looked in the direction of Grandmother Frannie's house. Even though Frannie had left the house to Annabelle, TJ would always think of it as their grandmother's. None of them spoke. The only sound was the tick, tick, tick as the motor cooled.

"Are you two all right?" Annabelle asked.

TJ hadn't realized it when they'd met her at the airport, but Chloe had flown in only thirty minutes before she had. Which meant that like her, she hadn't been to the house where they were raised since the funeral.

"It's like it was when we were kids," Annabelle said, as if trying to reassure them.

From the back seat, TJ glanced at her sister in the rearview mirror. All three of them knew the house would never be like that again. Not after their grandmother's secrets had been unearthed, so to speak.

"If you don't want to stay here, we can go out to Dawson's ranch," Annabelle said. "We have a standing invitation."

TJ smiled at that, seeing how happy her sister was to be back together with her high school sweetheart. "I'm good with staying in the house."

"Of course you are," Chloe said. "You write

murder mysteries." She sighed. "I am good with staying here too. I think it's what Grandmother would have wanted. But it's still weird. I can't believe the secrets our grandmother kept from us."

TJ chuckled. Frannie had been a tiny, sweet little woman who everyone said wouldn't hurt a fly. "Seems all those wild stories we thought she made up to entertain us had some truth in them."

"Imagine if she hadn't toned them down to PG," Annabelle said.

They all laughed and opened their car doors, the earlier tension gone. Getting the luggage out, they made their way up the shoveled path through the deep snow. *Christmas in Whitehorse*, TJ thought. The last time she'd left here, she'd been pretty sure she'd never be back. But as she breathed in the icy evening air, she knew she was exactly where she wanted to be right now.

Annabelle scooped up a handful of snow in her mitten and tossed it into the air over them before running toward the door, fearing payback. Both TJ and Chloe let out cries as ice crystals glittered in the silver evening before covering them from head to toe.

TJ shook the light snow from her long blond hair and laughed. It was good to see Annabelle like this. It had been a long time. Now, she was again that adventurous young girl who'd gotten stuck in the neighbor boy's tree house.

"I thought you'd want your old rooms," Annabelle was saying as they crossed the porch and she unlocked the door.

TJ hadn't known what to expect as the door swung open. Her grandmother had been a hoarder in her old age. The last time she'd seen this place—when she and Chloe had come up for the funeral—it had been so full of newspapers, magazines, knickknacks, old furniture and so much junk there were only paths through the house. Little had they known what was buried in there.

She stopped in the doorway, dumbstruck. The junk was gone. The walls were painted a nice pale gray, and the place looked warm and welcoming, complete with new furniture.

"Annabelle, you shouldn't have gone to so much trouble. We aren't staying that long," TJ said, shocked.

"It wasn't all me. Willie insisted on helping and I wasn't about to say no," Annabelle said. "You remember Dawson's mom. When she takes on a project... You have to see the kitchen. Dawson completely remodeled it."

TJ could only nod and follow her sister into the kitchen where their grandmother used to attempt to cook. She stopped in the doorway. This was the room where Annabelle had discovered her grandmother's biggest secret. It looked like any other kitchen in an older remodeled house.

"Remember the cookie jar where Frannie kept her grocery money?" her sister was saying. "I saved it."

Chloe had stepped in and was looking around, wide-eyed. "It's amazing." She met TJ's gaze. "Ghosts?"

"Gone," Annabelle said, and crossed her heart with her index finger. "No ghosts."

TJ thought ghosts were the least of her problems. "Did Willie help you with our rooms as well?"

"She did. Come on, I'll show you." Annabelle ran up the stairs. TJ and Chloe followed, whispering among themselves.

"She did a great job," Chloe was saying. "Remember what it was like?"

"Unfortunately, I do," TJ said. "Like a horror story."

"Or a thriller," Chloe whispered back. "Like the kind you write."

TJ didn't need the reminder.

Annabelle had stopped at Chloe's old room. They joined her. The room had been painted her favorite color, pale purple, and decorated to fit their investigative reporter sister's style.

"You do realize that this visit is temporary, right?" TJ asked. Annabelle didn't seem to hear her. Stepping down the hall, TJ stopped at a room she knew at once was hers. It was painted a pale yellow. A quilt of yellow-and-blue fabric lay on the antique white iron bed. There was a small white desk and chair to one side of the bed with a lamp and spot for her laptop. On the wall above it was a framed collage of her book covers.

"Do you like it?" Annabelle said behind her, sounding anxious.

"Oh, Annabelle." She turned to hug her sister, hoping to hide her discomfort. The last thing she wanted to see were her book covers right now. They reminded her of the threats from her True Fan, who had found fault with all of her latest plots—and even her covers.

"It's perfect."

Her sister seemed to relax. "Is this going to be all right?" she asked.

"It is, Belle," she said using a nickname for her littlest sister that she hadn't used in years. "I'm glad you kept Frannie's house."

"It was Dawson's idea. He bought it for a rental but he thought it would be nice for us to have it for when the two of you visit. After we're married, we'll build a house with guest rooms for you and Chloe when you come home. Then we'll either rent this house or sell it. But I like the idea of keeping it. At least for a while."

She loved her sister's enthusiasm, but she couldn't imagine visiting Whitehorse often. So she said nothing, just smiled and hugged her again.

Chloe came out of her room holding a framed photo of the three of them.

"Check this out," she said, wiping tears as she showed TJ a photo of the them when they were girls. "We were so cute."

"We are still cute," Annabelle said. "Let's go to Ray J's and get some barbecue. Then I'm thinking we should go to the Mint and celebrate."

"Whoa," Chloe said. "Barbecue, yes. Our old bar, no." She looked to TJ to back her up.

"How about we come back here, open the wine and make it a fairly early night," TJ said. "At least for today. It's been kind of a long day. But could we stop by the bookstore before it closes on the way to supper? I need to see if they have everything they need for my book signing."

"You're doing a book signing this close to Christmas?" Chloe said.

"Don't ask."

THE BOOKSTORE WAS actually a gift shop that carried her books because she was considered a local author. TJ stopped inside the door. It had been so long since she'd had her very first signing here. She remembered her excitement from the acceptance of her book to actually seeing her words in print. She'd been over the moon. She hadn't been able to quit staring at her book. The memory made her smile. Her dream had come true.

Her first book signing under this roof had been good. She'd known most everyone who'd waited in line to talk to her, wish her well, say they knew her when, and then get their book signed.

TJ hung on to that feeling for a moment before stepping in to look for the owner. Her sisters scattered throughout the store, oohing and aahing over this or that as she made her way to the books.

There were a dozen piled up next to an older

image of her along with some articles about her on poster board. She'd been interviewed so many times and freely told stories about her life, her dreams, her process.

She couldn't help but grimace at the memory of the tongue-lashing the New York City police officer had given her when she'd taken the threatening letters in to him.

"Look, there's nothing we can do," the cop said. "These aren't the first threats you've gotten, nor will they be the last. You writers," he said with a shake of his head. "I checked out your web page, your social media. Your whole life, everything about you from what you ate for dinner last night to your favorite color, is out there for public consumption. You put your life out there to promote yourself and your books. So..." He shrugged. "What do you expect?"

Not seeing the owner, TJ stepped away from the book display and the poster of her as she heard more people come into the store on a gust of cold air. She hadn't gone far when she heard a deep male voice ask if they had TJ St. Clair's latest book.

She turned and froze. The man was a good six foot five, shoulders as wide as an ax handle and arms bulging with muscle. But it was the dark curly hair at his collar, the baseball cap and the sheepskin coat that sliced into her heart like a knife.

The owner of the store was telling him about the book signing the following day and how TJ had grown up right here in Whitehorse. "Here, you'll want a bookmark. The signing is at 10 a.m. Best come early because it will fill up fast. Tessa Jane hasn't done a signing here in years so we're all very excited."

"Yes, I don't want to miss that," he said, his voice a low rumble.

TJ felt glued to the floor. This was the man who'd pulled her back from the speeding truck—and possibly pushed her to start with—early this morning in New York City and was now here in Whitehorse? Even as she told herself it couldn't possibly be the same man, she knew in her heart it was. The only way he could have gotten here this quickly was if he'd already had a flight out of the city. As if he'd already known where she was going.

Just then he turned and she saw the dark beard on his granite jaw. A pair of piercing blue eyes pinned her to the spot. What she saw, what she felt, it came in a jumble of emotions so strong and unsettling that she turned and ran.

Chapter Four

TJ stumbled blindly out the door and around the corner. She leaned against the brick wall and tried to catch her breath. Her life felt out of control. *She* felt out of control. She'd never had a reaction like that and now, shivering out in the cold, she wondered what had possessed her.

She couldn't even explain her response to the man. What had she sensed that had her running out into the cold? She shivered, hugging herself as she thought of those blue eyes and the look in them. It was as if he could see into her soul. She knew that was pure foolishness, but how else could she explain her reaction?

"What in the world!" cried her sister Annabelle as she found her leaning against the outside of the building. Chloe came running up a moment later. "What happened?"

TJ couldn't speak. She shook her head and fought tears. But it was useless. She began to cry, letting out all the frustration and fear that she'd been holding in the past six months.

Her sisters rushed to her, drawing her to them as they exchanged looks of concern. "Let's get her over to the coffee shop," she heard Annabelle say.

TJ tried to pull herself together. At the sound of a truck engine, she looked up. To her horror, she saw that it was the man she'd just seen in the gift store driving by slowly. She couldn't see those blue eyes, but she could feel them on her.

"Who is that man?" TJ asked on a ragged breath before the truck disappeared down the street.

Her sisters turned to look.

"I saw him in the gift shop." Chloe shook her head. "I have never seen him before that," she said with a shrug.

TJ had expected Annabelle to say the same thing and was surprised when her sister said, "The mountain man?"

"You know him?" TJ asked as the pickup continued down the street. The truck, she saw with surprise, had a local license plate on it. How was that possible? It was the same man she'd seen in New York City earlier today. But how could that be? She was losing her mind.

"His name is Silas Walker. He moved here about six months ago," Annabelle was saying. *He'd moved here six months ago?* That was about the time TJ started getting the letters from True Fan. "He keeps to himself. Has a place in the Little Rockies."

"You can bet he's running from something,"

Chloe said. "Probably has a rap sheet as long as his muscled arm."

"Do you always have to be so suspicious?" Annabelle said with a sigh.

"Seriously, he's either a criminal or an ex-cop."

"One extreme or the other?" Annabelle grumbled. "Sweetie," she said, turning back to TJ. "You're shivering. Let's get you into the coffee shop."

It wasn't until they were seated, cups of hot coffee in their hands, that her sisters asked what was going on.

She wished she knew. Fearing that she was letting her paranoia get to her, she didn't know what to say.

"TJ?" Chloe prompted.

"She's finally getting some color back into her face," Annabelle said. "Just give her a minute."

She took a sip of the hot coffee. It burned

all the way down, but began to warm her ice-cold center.

"Tell us what's going on," Chloe said. "Tessa Jane, you looked like you saw a ghost back there. Do you know that man?"

Looking up at them, she knew she couldn't keep it from them any longer.

It all came pouring out about the fan that at first was so complimentary but soon became more critical, making suggestions that when she didn't take them became angry.

"Who do you think it is? Probably some aspiring writer with too many rejections who's angry at you because you got published and she didn't?" Annabelle asked.

"Or maybe another writer who's jealous of your success?" Chloe added.

TJ shook her head. "That's just it. I have no idea. It could be just a reader who doesn't like the direction my books have taken. I'm not even sure if it is a man or a woman. I'm not the first writer to run into this problem. Readers bond with an author. They have expectations when they pick up one of your books. If you don't meet those expectations…"

"What? They threaten to kill you?" Chloe cried. "Have you gone to the police?"

She told them what had happened. "The officer was right. My entire life is out there in the cloud. When I was starting out, I hadn't realized that everything I said to the press or online would be available online forever. At first I was just so excited to be published. I never dreamed…" She shook her head.

"I can't believe the police blame you," Chloe said.

Annabelle agreed. "Though I have to admit, it goes with the business. I ran into this with modeling. Once you're out there, you become public property."

"That's ridiculous," Chloe said.

"Don't tell me that you haven't run into this as a reporter," TJ said.

"People storming in angry about something I've written? Of course," Chloe said. "It's part of the job. You can't please everyone. But if you're being threatened…"

"What are you going to do?" Annabelle asked.

She shook her head. "The police officer I talked to said I should ride it out. That the fan would get tired of harassing me. But I'm worried with this new book that True Fan isn't going to like it at all. After seeing that man…"

"You think it's him, your True Fan," Chloe said. "The one who looks like a mountain man?"

TJ sighed and told them what had happened only that morning on the street in front of her apartment. "He saved me, but did he? I felt someone push me in front of that truck. If he hadn't grabbed me…" She saw her sisters exchange a doubtful look. "I know it doesn't seem likely that they are the same person, but…" She halted for a moment. "I swear it's the same man. I…feel it."

"Okay, it's a stretch," Chloe said. "But I suppose it's possible. You were in New York this morning and now you're here. Why couldn't it be the same for him?"

"He could have even been on the same flight," Annabelle said. "You flew first class, right? He probably flew coach. And since you didn't have any luggage to claim…"

"Okay, it's not that much of a coincidence if he is the same man," Chloe said. "It doesn't make him True Fan though."

"Right, it isn't like he followed you here," Annabelle said. "He's been living here for the past six months."

"Six months," TJ said in a whisper. "That's how long I've been getting the letters from True Fan."

SILAS DROVE TOWARD the Little Rockies, anxious to get to his cabin. As he drove, he contemplated what had happened back at the gift shop. It didn't make a lot of sense and he was a man who prided himself on making sense out of situations.

At least he'd been right about one thing. TJ St. Clair had been headed home for the holidays. When he'd realized that, he'd been looking forward to meeting her. But after what had happened back there…

She'd run out of the shop in tears. Because of him? Or someone else she saw in the store? Odd behavior. He considered that it might have something to do with what had happened this morning in New York. A scare like that would make anyone jumpy. He frowned to himself, wondering again about her near accident this morning.

Was she merely jostled? Had someone purposely pushed her?

He shook his head, reprimanding himself for not leaving his job behind along with the suspicions that went with it. He was in Montana now. He'd bought this place outside of Whitehorse in the Little Rockies so he could get away from his stressful, dangerous, always unpredictable job.

Here, he did so much physical labor that all of that ugliness was forgotten—at least for a while. Here, he'd put that world as far away from him as he could.

And yet you still read thrillers. Not just anyone's. You read her books.

He laughed as he drove toward the mountains. That's because she was the reason he'd moved here. After reading TJ's books, he'd been curious about Montana, curious about the wild prairie, the endless sky, the wide-open places that she talked about in her books. Once he saw the area, he was hooked. She had always mentioned the Little Rockies so of course that's where he went when he was looking for land. While he loved the prairie, he also wanted a hideaway like the lawless days when Kid Curry and Butch Cassidy and the Sundance Kid roamed this area.

He'd bought into the mystique because of TJ St. Clair and because of her books, but he'd never dreamed he'd get a chance to meet her here in her home state. Which was why he couldn't miss her book signing tomorrow. He knew even before he turned onto the snow-packed road that led up into the mountains to his cabin that nothing was going to keep him away. He realized that he'd been wanting to meet her for far too long.

TJ LISTENED TO her sisters chatting, knowing they were trying to get her mind off True Fan and her book signing tomorrow. She smiled and nodded and added a word or two when required as she tried to enjoy her barbecued pulled pork. It was delicious and she was hungry after a long day with little real food.

But she couldn't keep her mind off the man she'd seen at the gift shop. The mountain man. Her True Fan?

She thought back to the first letter. It had been so complimentary. The writer had loved the book, sounding surprised as if not a thriller reader. She tried to reconcile that first letter with the more recent bitter, hateful ones she'd been getting. She couldn't square them anymore than she could the man she'd seen first in New York and now in her local gift shop asking about her book.

The first letter had been like so many of the others that she had hardly noticed it.

"You really need to hire someone to answer these," her friend Mica had said when she'd seen the stack TJ had been working her way through on that day six months ago.

"I've thought about it, but I'd rather not answer them than have someone else do it for me. I know that sounds crazy."

"No, I get it." Mica had opened a couple of the letters and begun to read them. "Aww, these are so sweet. They love you. This one is from a woman who is almost ninety. She wants you to write faster." Her friend had laughed. "Oh and this one is long." She'd watched Mica skim it. "Good heavens, do people often tell you their entire life histories?"

TJ had nodded. "They want to share their lives with me because they feel they know me from my books. You can see why I try to answer as many of the fan letters as I can. Unfortunately I can't answer them all. I just hope they understand."

After her friend left, TJ had answered as many of the letters as she'd had time for since she had a book deadline looming. She *always* had a deadline looming.

That part she didn't mind. She loved writing

the stories. It was the other things that ate up her time that she hated. There were always art forms that needed to be filled out describing her story, her characters, suggesting scenes for the cover.

Then there were the many edits and proposals that needed to be written. Add to that the blogs and promotion requests. It was a wonder she ever had time to write the books.

She had been thinking about that when she'd picked up one more fan letter to possibly answer. The first thing she had noticed was that there was no return address on the envelope. She hadn't thought too much about it since often the readers would put their addresses inside their letters.

Slicing open the envelope, she'd pulled out the folded unlined discolored paper. She remembered holding it up to the light, wondering how old it was to have turned this color. The letter had been typed on what appeared to be a manual typewriter. TJ had an old heavy Royal she'd picked up and kept in her office only as decoration. She'd always been impressed that Ernest Hemingway had written on a manual typewriter, since she doubted she would be writing books if it weren't for the ease of computers.

Dear Ms. St. Clair

I've never written an author before. I guess there is a first time for everything.

I recently checked out your first book from the local library. It was quite pleasurable to read. You clearly have talent. I was surprised when I started reading and couldn't put it down. I definitely enjoyed your descriptions of Montana and the country around your "fictitious" small town.

I'm actually looking forward to your next book,

Your True Fan so far

TJ had laughed. The reader certainly hadn't thought he or she was going to like it. It had pleased her that her True Fan had been surprised and willing to try another one of her books. Maybe next time the person would purchase one rather than wait to get it at the library.

She had looked to see if there was a name or an address. Apparently the reader didn't require an answer. She'd tossed the letter in the trash since long ago she'd given up keeping all the fan mail. She'd thought nothing more of it.

That, she realized now, had been her first mistake. There might have been fingerprints on that first letter before things went south.

Chapter Five

"I want to read the letters you got from this so-called fan of yours," Chloe said once they were back at the house and alone. Their sister had gone to see her fiancé, Dawson Rogers, promising to come back before all the wine was gone. "Something tells me they are much more threatening than what you told Annabelle."

"I didn't bring them with me," TJ said. "I didn't even save the first few." But she remembered them and often saw them in her sleep, waking in a cold sweat, her heart pounding.

Dear Ms. St. Clair

I was so disappointed with your last book. To think a tree was killed to make the paper that book was printed on… You should be ashamed.

I expect each book to be better than the last. I don't think that's unreasonable. In my last letter, I made some suggestions as far as the plot and character development.

Clearly, you dismissed those suggestions. Maybe you think you know more about writing than I do. Since my opinion doesn't count, you won't be surprised to hear that I don't trust you as a narrator.

I'm your only honest fan. If this is the way you treat a true fan, I hate to think how you treat your other readers.

You have really let me down. We might have to do something about that, don't you think?

Your only True Fan

She'd thought that would be the last time she'd hear from that reader. She didn't remember a suggestion for a book that True Fan had claimed to have sent her. Readers often thought she should do books about various secondary characters from her novels. One even suggested getting a woman out of the criminally insane ward of a hospital so she could find her true love. What readers didn't seem to realize was that those decisions weren't always up to her—even if she was inclined to do a certain character's story.

She'd thrown True Fan's letter away—just as she had the first one—and moved on to a letter by a woman who would love a signed book sent to her sister for her birthday. Her sister loved TJ's books and was laid up after a car wreck. The sister's name was Rickey. The reader had said that the sister was a huge fan.

TJ had picked up one of her books and signed

it: *Rickey, Happy Birthday. Hope you're well soon, Best, TJ St. Clair.*

She put it with the letter in the pile to be mailed, only vaguely remembering that it went to a post office box in Laramie, Wyoming.

After that, she'd gone back to writing her book and forgotten both letters.

That had been her second mistake, though she'd had no way of knowing it at the time. It wasn't until she received the next letter from True Fan:

Dear TJ St. Clair

You really aren't as bright or as talented as I first thought. Actually, I'm amazed you make any money at this. A person you don't know from Adam tells you a hard-luck story and you send them a book? You are so gullible. But "Rickey" thanks you. Tee Hee. I'm feeling so much better and I like having a book that you touched.

Unfortunately, your books are getting worse. I didn't think that was possible. I told you what to do, but you just keep ignoring me. Because you think you're so much smarter than me, more talented? You keep making this mistake and we'll see who is smarter.

Your True Fan until The End

"Believe me," TJ told her sister now. "I've read them numerous times. I can't tell if they are from a man or a woman. They could be from *anyone*. Anyone who owns an old manual typewriter."

"Well, they have you running scared, so you must believe the threats are real," her sister said.

"The last one promised that True Fan would be seeing me soon and unless I apologized for ignoring the advice the person had been giving me, I was going to die like one of the characters in my book," TJ said. "True Fan said I could pick which character and which death and kill myself because it would be less painful than if a fan had to stop me from writing by killing me."

Chloe shivered. "That sounds like more than a threat. The police didn't take that seriously?"

TJ poured herself a glass of wine, her hands shaking. "Even if True Fan had said he or she was going to kill me, there is no return address. The postmarks have been from all over the country. Where would they begin looking for this person? We don't know if it's a man or woman. So until True Fan actually makes good on these threats..." She got to her feet. "I hate talking about this."

"This man we saw earlier, you realize it's a long shot that he's the same one from New York, but I could do some checking. Annabelle said his name is Silas Walker." She ran upstairs, returned with her laptop and began to tap on the keys.

TJ was thinking how nice it was to have an investigative reporter in the family when Chloe let out a sharp breath and looked up. "What?"

"He was one of New York's finest, but left a year ago after being caught in some kind of internal sting investigation."

"What kind of investigation?" TJ asked around the lump in her throat.

Chloe shook her head. "Dirty cops. He apparently was never arrested. All they said was misconduct that betrayed the public's trust. That could be anything from lying to cheating on overtime or much worse. Here's the kicker: he was rehired a month later but then quit." She looked up from her computer. "This guy could be dangerous."

"What guy could be dangerous?" Annabelle asked as she came through the front door on a gust of winter wind. TJ and Chloe shared a look. "Are you talking about the Mountain Man?"

"He's an ex-cop who was fired at one point," Chloe said. "I was saying he could be dangerous."

"Why was he fired?" their sister asked as she shrugged out of her coat, hung it up and joined them. She poured herself a glass of wine. Her cheeks were already flushed. From the cold? Or from her visit with Dawson Rogers?

"Let's not talk about this," TJ said. "Tell us about you and Dawson."

Annabelle shook her head. "If you really think this man is dangerous then you need to cancel your book signing tomorrow."

"Bad idea," Chloe said. "She'll be perfectly safe at the gift shop with us and half the town there. This is her chance to find out if he's this True Fan who's been sending her the threatening letters."

"You really think it's him?" Annabelle asked.

"First I'm shoved from behind in front of a speeding delivery truck, he saves me, then shows up in Whitehorse and I find out that he moved here six months ago—about the same time I started getting the threatening letters. What are the chances that he's *not* True Fan?" She shuddered at the memory of those blue eyes. She'd felt strangely drawn to him at the same time she'd felt afraid.

"What does she do if he *does* show up at the book signing tomorrow?" Annabelle demanded of Chloe. "Just ask him if he's her True Fan?"

Chloe groaned. "She'll play it cool. We'll be there. If he is this crazed fan, he won't do anything at the signing, but he might say something that gives him away. Once we know for sure then we go to the sheriff."

"TJ play it cool?" her youngest sister said

with a laugh. "No offense, but if today was any indication—"

"I can do it." TJ nodded with more enthusiasm than she felt. She had to. This had to end because she couldn't take anymore. If it didn't, she feared True Fan would end it the way the letters had promised. "Maybe he won't even show."

"I wouldn't hold my breath," Chloe said. "If it's him, he'll want to get as close to you as he can. He's been taunting you. Now he'll want you to know just how close he is."

As if TJ didn't already know the psychology behind a person like this. She wrote about them all the time. If this man was her True Fan, he didn't just want her to know how close he was. He wanted her to know how easy it would be for him to get to her. For the past six months, this had been leading up to the moment when she faced her killer—just like in one of her books.

Chapter Six

When TJ woke the next morning, she was shocked to see how late it was. She hurriedly showered and dressed. When she came downstairs, dressed for her signing, Annabelle handed her a cup of coffee and a donut.

She took the coffee, declined the donut and watched as Annabelle ate it.

"I love not being a model anymore," her sister said, smiling with a little sugar glaze on her lips before she licked it away.

TJ couldn't help smiling as well. Her sister looked great, not skinny and pale like she had when she'd been a top model. "I need to get to my signing."

"We're going with you," Chloe said, coming out of the kitchen. "Are you nervous?"

What did she think? She'd never been good at book signings. Probably because she'd never wanted the attention. She'd only wanted to write the stories that were in her head. Little had she known the rest that was required of a published author. TJ knew she was naive to think that she could simply lock herself away in a room somewhere and do what she loved.

When her editor had told her that she needed to be more of a presence on social media, she'd actually thought about quitting the publishing business.

But she couldn't quit writing. When she'd take a break, the longest she could go was three days before she started writing in her sleep. The characters would start talking and she'd have to get their stories out. She loved that part.

TJ remembered how surprised she'd been when she found out that not everyone had stories going in their heads. She'd asked the person, "Well, then what do you think about when you're in the shower or driving?" The answer had been, "I've never thought about it. Something I'm sure, but not stories."

It had also surprised her when other writers had told her that their characters didn't talk to them. Well, hers certainly did. Soon the ones from her next book would be nagging at her to begin writing again.

"Come on," Chloe said, "or we're going to be late."

TJ wished they could just get into Annabelle's SUV—she'd traded her sports car for something more practical for Montana—and hit the road. She thought she could and not look back at this point in her life.

There was already a line at the gift shop when they arrived. TJ couldn't help looking for the mountain man, but with a sigh of relief, she didn't see him. Maybe after yesterday, he wouldn't show up.

"Park in the back," she'd instructed her sister.

"You aren't getting cold feet, are you?" Chloe asked.

"I always do but nothing like I have right now." They entered the back door. TJ dropped off her coat and purse in the stockroom and took a moment to compose herself. *You've done this dozens of other times. You can do this.*

But none of the other times were like this.

Stepping out of the back, she headed for the table that had been set up for her along with a chair and a huge stack of her books. The owner hustled over to see if she needed water, coffee, anything at all.

"A bottle of water would be wonderful," TJ said, her throat already dry as she felt eyes on her from the line of people waiting a few yards away. She tried to smile as she slid into the chair and picked up one of the pens the store owner had thoughtfully left for her.

"Here's your water," said a familiar voice.

TJ turned to see a dark-haired woman her age. "Joyce?" She couldn't help her surprise. She hadn't seen Joyce Mason since high school. Joyce had been voted the girl most likely to end up behind bars. It had been a play on words, since Joyce had been wild— and also a drinker who was known to make out with guys in the alley behind the Mint Bar.

"You work here now?" TJ asked, feeling the need to say something into the silence. Joyce was thinner than in high school, but wore the same shag hairdo and pretty much the same expression, one of boredom. The only thing different was that she sported a few more tattoos.

"Does it surprise you that I read?" Joyce asked.

"No." She let out a nervous laugh. "As a writer, I'm delighted."

"Yes, we all know you're a writer." Joyce put down the bottle of water and walked off.

TJ was still reeling a little from Joyce's attitude when she heard a squeal and looked up to see another familiar face. Dorothy "Dot" Crest came running up to her all smiles.

"I can't believe it!" Dot cried. "I just had to say hi. I'll get in line," she assured the waiting crowd. "I definitely want one of your books. I've read them all." She leaned closer. "They are so scary and yet I can't put them down." She laughed. "This is so exciting."

With that she rushed back toward the end of the line. As she did, she said hello to people she knew. Dot knew almost everyone it seemed.

"Ready?" the owner asked, coming up to

tell her again how delighted they were to have her here.

Was she ready? She felt off-balance and the signing hadn't even begun. Normally, TJ was more organized. She'd barely remembered to grab a few bookmarks as they'd left the house. She hadn't even thought about a pen. That showed just how nervous she was.

She smiled up at the first woman in line. She looked familiar, but for a moment TJ couldn't come up with her name. That was the problem at book signings. The names of people she knew even really well would slip her mind.

"Just sign it to me," a person would say.

She often used the trick, "Would you mind spelling your name for me?"

That didn't always work. One woman who was so excited, telling everyone how long she'd known TJ, made her draw a blank. When she'd asked her to spell her name, the woman recoiled and said, "It's Pat."

TJ had been so embarrassed, but there hadn't been time to explain how often her mind went blank at these events, even with the names of her closest friends. So she never saw Pat again.

Now the older woman with the dyed-brown hair standing in front of the desk said, "You probably don't remember me."

For a moment, TJ didn't. She looked familiar. Really familiar, but...

"I'm not surprised given how much you didn't pay attention in class."

Bingo. "Of course I remember you, Mrs. Brown. I had you for English in high school." Annabelle had told her that the woman had only recently retired after having a minor stroke. "Would you like me to sign this to you?" she asked her former teacher.

"Of course. But you probably don't know my first name. It's Ester."

She signed the book, stuck in a bookmark and handed it to the older woman.

Ester Brown hesitated. "Just the other day I told my husband I wasn't the least bit surprised when I heard you were writing books." She hugged the book to her. "You were never at a loss for words in my class." With that she turned and walked away.

TJ frowned. Hadn't Annabelle told her that Mrs. Brown's husband had died?

One after another new and old readers stepped up and TJ signed their books, visited and moved on to the next one. She was surprised how many people had turned out. But the last time she had signed a book in her hometown had been her first one years ago.

"Hi, TJ," said one of the men from the line. She'd seen him, but hadn't paid much attention. She was looking for the mountain man. But if Silas Walker was planning to attend the signing, he hadn't shown so far, and another five minutes and she would be done. The line had dwindled, she realized with relief.

Her hand hurt from signing books and smiling and trying to remember faces she hadn't seen in years.

Now as she looked at this man, his name suddenly came to her. "Tommy Harwood."

"Tom," he corrected. He seemed surprised that she remembered him. He'd been one of those on the fringe. He'd been an average student, an outsider. He'd been invisible—just like TJ. While her sisters had been popular, TJ was a dreamer who preferred to be off by herself with her head in a book.

Now Tommy was getting a little bald. From the jacket he was wearing, she saw that he worked at the local auto shop.

"Do you want it signed to you?" she asked as she opened a book and lifted her pen expectantly.

"Sure, as long as it's to Tom."

She nodded and signed *To Tom, Enjoy, TJ St. Clair*. It was the best she could do given that she didn't think she'd spoken more than a dozen words to Tommy over the years. No matter what Mrs. Brown said, she wasn't the talkative one in English class. TJ realized she must have her confused with Annabelle. Great.

"Are you in town long?" Tommy asked quietly.

"Just for the holidays." She handed him the book.

He continued to stare at her. "You're probably busy, but if you ever want to get a cup of coffee…"

"Thank you. That's sounds nice. I'll let you know."

He nodded. "I should let you get to your other fans."

She watched him walk away for a moment, trying to shake off the odd feeling he'd given her.

"I love your books," a woman said as she quickly took Tommy's place and it continued.

As the line dwindled, she began to relax. She loved her readers and was reminded of the time before her first sale. She'd been writing short stories. That's when she'd gotten her very first fan letter. The magazine reader had said she should be writing books. She'd framed that first letter and put in on her wall. It had given her hope each time she looked at it during the writing of her first book.

She could smile at the memory. There'd been so many days when she didn't think she could finish an entire book. It had felt overwhelming. Add to that the fear that it wasn't good enough, that everyone would hate it, that it would be rejected.

And it was. Her first book was still in the bottom of her closet where it would remain, never to be published. But that first book had given her hope not only that she could finish a book, but also that she could write a better one.

And she had. A book a year for the past

seven years, all of them published, each doing better than the last. She remembered the thrill of her fourth book making the *New York Times* list.

She'd heard of authors who'd treated themselves with trips to Europe or purchased new cars after making the list. She'd gone for a walk, grinning the whole way, and on impulse had treated herself to a hot fudge sundae. It was as decadent as she ever got. Restraint in everything, that was TJ St. Clair, aka Tessa Jane Clementine. Those words could have been stitched and hung on her wall.

She'd always been like that. Holding back, never letting herself go. It drove her sister Annabelle crazy.

"Don't you ever just want to let loose? Do something crazy? Take a chance?"

"I might want to, but I don't," had been her answer. The truth was she'd never been brave or daring. That huge hot fudge sundae? It had made her sick and had been a good reminder of why she used restraint in all things.

No, her heroine in her books, Constance Ryan, was the one who did crazy, brave and daring things. Constance loved defying the odds. And for so long, TJ had loved writing about her—living through her.

As she finished signing a young woman's book, TJ saw him. The mountain man, Silas Walker, had just come in the door and was headed her way.

Chapter Seven

Silas was a little concerned about what kind of reception he might get. Because of his size and the way he looked, especially during his time in Montana when he was "roughin' it," he tended to scare little children. Lately he'd been working undercover, so his beard was longer than usual. He'd let his hair grow as well.

But the woman who wrote these murder mysteries? Come on, TJ didn't scare that easily, did she?

He guessed he was about to find out as he headed for the table where she had just finished signing a book. There were still several books left, he noticed with relief. He'd run late today because of the snowstorm in the mountains last night. He'd barely been able to get his pickup out. But he wasn't about to miss purchasing a signed book from TJ St. Clair today.

When she spotted him approaching, he had to admit, she looked like a deer in headlights. It perplexed him. She couldn't possibly have thought that he was the one who pushed her into the street yesterday. He'd been the one who saved her.

"Hello," he said as he reached the table. "I can't tell you how excited I am that I didn't miss your signing." His gaze locked with hers and he was shocked to see that her eyes weren't blue, but a languid sea green that took his breath away for a moment. Her blond hair framed a face that he'd memorized, since he'd looked at the black-and-white photograph on the cover jacket so many times.

She'd intrigued him from the first time he'd picked up one of her books. He normally didn't read thrillers. Hell, his life was one. No, he couldn't remember what had possessed him.

He'd opened one of her books to the first page and started reading. Before he knew it, he was on page 30. By then, he was hooked and knew he wasn't walking out of that bookstore without that book.

It wasn't until he'd finished it that he saw TJ's photo. He'd actually thought the book had been written by a man. He remembered smiling. He liked surprises and this woman had surprised him and intrigued him.

Now he watched her pick up one of the hardcover books at her elbow and open it with trembling fingers. That he made her nervous surprised him even given the way she'd acted yesterday. In her books, the characters were so gutsy. He liked to believe that TJ possessed—

if not all of her character Constance's gutsiness—then at least some of it. The last thing he'd expected to see in her eyes was fear.

"Who would you like me to sign it to?" she asked, her voice breaking.

He knelt down, realizing he was towering over her, although he suspected that wasn't the problem. "Silas." He spelled his name and watched her write it out in her neat penmanship. "I can't tell you what a thrill this is. From the first time I picked up one of your books, I wanted to meet the woman behind them."

He saw her pen falter on the page. Those sea green eyes came up to meet his. He smiled and saw her shiver. She quickly looked down and hurriedly signed "Enjoy" and her name. Well, not her name exactly. TJ St. Clair he'd learned was her pen name. Her legal name was Tessa Jane Clementine.

She handed him the book. "I hope you like it." Her voice was throaty, almost a whisper.

He saw that there was no one behind him since he'd caught her at the end of the signing. "I have enjoyed your books so much. I just had to tell you that." He started to rise, but stopped. "I know this is probably out of line, but is there some reason I make you so nervous?"

She parted her lips as if to speak. She had a great mouth, he noticed. She quickly closed it for a moment before she spoke. "Is there a reason you should make me nervous?"

"Not that I know of," he said. "When I saw that you were going to be signing books here, I had hoped…" He shook his head. "You probably don't accept dates from your readers. I don't blame you. It's just that reading your books…well, I feel I know you. That must sound crazy. But you're why I ended up building a cabin here." He shrugged. "I'm sorry, you're probably anxious to leave." He smiled as he rose. "Maybe we'll see each other around town. Thank you so much for this," he said, looking down at the book in his hands. "I'll treasure it." He met her gaze. "It was wonderful meeting you."

TJ SAT STUNNED as she watched Silas Walker stride over to the checkout counter and pay for his book. She kept thinking about his intense blue eyes and his disarming smile. He knew that he made him nervous. Had he been enjoying that, or was he trying to make her less nervous?

"Well," Chloe whispered as she rushed over to her. "Is it him?"

For a moment she couldn't speak. "I have no idea. Apparently, he was going to ask me out but changed his mind."

Annabelle appeared to hear the last part. She let out a laugh. *"So he just wanted a date?"*

"He gave you no indication that he might be True Fan?" Chloe demanded.

"None." And yet… She remembered the way he'd looked into her eyes. What had he been looking for? She shuddered and let out a sigh. "I am so glad this book signing is over."

"He was at your table for quite a while," Chloe said, not letting it go. "What else did he say?"

"I don't know," TJ said. "My brain was on spin cycle. He said he felt as if he knew me from my books and that was probably crazy. Oh, and that I was the reason he built a cabin here. That is, my books were."

Annabelle's eyes went wide. "That doesn't sound good, but you don't live here anymore. You live in New York City, so…"

"He didn't mention saving your life in the city yesterday morning?" Chloe asked.

"No," TJ said with a shake of her head. "I

should have asked him but my suspicions all seemed so ludicrous at the time. He kept looking at me as if…" She shook her head. As if he really just wanted to ask her out? Or something else? She had no idea.

"You knew your True Fan could be charming, right?" Chloe asked. "Maybe you should have accepted the date."

"No!" Annabelle cried. "What if he is… True Fan?"

"Well, he changed his mind about asking me out, so the point is moot," she pointed out. "Tommy Harwood asked me out though." Her sisters gave her a blank look, which confirmed that Tommy had gone through high school as invisible as she had been.

When she described him, Chloe said, "I do remember him vaguely."

"Kind of getting bald guy with the little potbelly?" Annabelle asked.

"That's him. He works at the auto shop."

They both quickly lost interest in him.

"I saw Dot. She hasn't changed a bit," Chloe said.

"Joyce Mason apparently works here," TJ said, keeping her voice down. She thought Joyce might be hiding nearby listening. "She was a little strange."

Chloe put an arm around her as she got to her feet to leave. "You survived it."

She smiled. She had. But she was no closer to finding out if one of the people who'd come through the line was True Fan.

"I say we go have some lunch," Annabelle said.

"It's that or head straight to the Mint Bar," Chloe said. "Up to you, Tessa Jane."

"Didn't someone say food?" Annabelle asked innocently. "I'm starved."

Chloe looked to TJ and said, "Food. I've never seen you this thin."

"Yes, we'll get you some good Montana eats

and fatten you right up," Annabelle agreed. "How about some chicken-fried steak?"

TJ felt her stomach roil at the thought. "Yum."

Her sisters laughed as they headed out the door. It was a wonderful sound that felt like a much-needed salve. She told herself that her True Fan hadn't been in Whitehorse today, hadn't come through the line, hadn't gone home with her latest book.

And yet she couldn't help but think about each and every one of the people who'd come through the line, including the young woman who'd been right before Silas Walker. TJ had been distracted, but now that she remembered…

"I signed a book for Nellie Doll," she said as they started up the street.

Chloe stopped, coming up short. "Lanell? I didn't see her in the line."

"She sent her niece to get it for her," TJ said.

"The niece had me sign it 'to Nellie, just like old times.'"

"That is kind of creepy, isn't it?" Chloe said. "You and Nellie weren't friends."

"No," TJ said. "Far from it." She tried to shake off the memory.

"You aren't thinking that Nellie..." Annabelle was walking backward in front of them, looking from TJ to Chloe and back again.

"That she's True Fan?" Chloe shook her head. "Anyway, didn't you say that the letters had been sent from all over the country? I'm betting Nellie's never been out of the county."

TJ nodded, remembering the girl Nellie had been in high school. She couldn't imagine that she'd want to drop so much money on a hardcover book, especially TJ's.

She tried not to think about True Fan. She had so many amazing readers. Why did one fan have to spoil it? What bothered her was that she really didn't know whether True Fan was a man or a woman. She'd had several women murderers in her books. In fact, in the book she'd just signed, the antagonist was a woman.

Chapter Eight

TJ woke with a headache after a night of weird dreams. She took a couple of OTC painkiller tablets after her shower. She was not looking forward to her interview with a reporter from the *Billings Gazette* later this morning.

As she dressed, she could hear her sisters already downstairs in the kitchen. Opening her bedroom door, she followed the rich, wonderful scent of coffee down the stairs.

She couldn't help smiling to herself. There was something so comforting about being back in this house with her sisters. Just the sound of them lightened her step as well as her heart. As she walked into the kitchen, she headed straight for the cupboard where she knew she would find a mug.

"Good morning!" Annabelle called from the table, where she and Chloe were already sitting with their coffee. "It's a beautiful day."

TJ blinked as she looked outside to see the sun shining on the new snow, making it glitter blindingly. "Were you always this cheerful in the morning?" she asked her as she took a seat at the table.

"Don't you hate morning people?" Chloe said, and grinned, since she was one as well.

"I thought we'd get a Christmas tree today," Annabelle said with unusual jubilance. "Willie saved some of Grandma Frannie's ornaments from the trip to the dump. We could decorate the tree later, and I need to do some Christmas shopping."

TJ could see what her sister was trying to

do—get her mind off True Fan and yesterday's book signing.

"Is there a place to buy a tree in town?" Chloe asked.

"Don't be silly," Annabelle said with a laugh. "We're going to take a picnic lunch and go up into the mountains and cut one. I found an ax in the garage."

"Ax?" Chloe cried.

"The Little Rockies?" TJ said, and both sisters turned to look at her.

"Why do I detect a strange excitement in those three words?" Chloe asked. "You aren't thinking what I think you're thinking."

"Of course not," TJ said. "It's just been so long since I've been up there." Both sisters were studying her. "Come on, he isn't True Fan."

"He said you were the reason he moved here," Chloe reminded her.

"Yes, but a lot of my readers say they feel

as if they're in Montana when they read one of my books and they can't wait to visit," she pointed out. "It's not that unusual."

"This one *moved* here," Chloe said.

"So you really don't think he's the one?" Annabelle asked suspiciously.

"He did nothing to indicate that he was anything more than a normal fan," TJ said truthfully. "So," she said, getting to her feet. "I'll pack the lunch. Let's go to the mountains and get a tree." She started at the knock on the door.

"I wonder who that is," Annabelle said as she went to answer.

TJ heard her laugh. "You're delivering mail door-to-door now?"

As she stepped out of the kitchen, TJ saw the woman hand her sister a letter. "You got mail," the woman said with a laugh as she looked past Annabelle to TJ. "Fan mail. Our own famous author. I tell people I know you—well, know that you used to live here—and they don't believe me."

All TJ could do was nod and smile as her heart sank. She felt all the color leave her face as Annabelle thanked the woman and closed the door.

"Carol from the post office," her sister was saying. "She said this came for you yesterday and since you don't have a post office box, she decided to drop it by. How's that for service? TJ?" Annabelle had seen that she'd gone pale.

Chloe took the envelope from Annabelle by the corner. "I'm sure there aren't any prints, but..." She held it out to TJ.

She didn't reach for it. Even from where she stood, she could see the typewritten address. Any other city and the letter would have ended up in a dead file because it had no return address and was addressed only to TJ St. Clair, Whitehorse, Montana. Another joy of living in a small Montana town.

"Aren't you going to open it?" Annabelle asked.

TJ couldn't find the words to speak.

"I'll open it," Chloe said, and walked into the kitchen to get a sharp knife. She carefully opened the letter, using the point of the knife to unfold the discolored paper.

How had the fan known she would be here? TJ groaned inwardly. Her fan knew she was in Whitehorse. Of course her fan knew; she'd just had a book signing. Not to mention she'd been recognized at the airport. That person had put it up on social media. Everyone in the world with a smartphone knew she was in Whitehorse—especially True Fan.

"The writer mailed it to you in Whitehorse, Montana," Chloe said. "So True Fan knew you were here. Only in a small town like this would you have gotten it," she said, voicing what TJ had just been thinking.

"Remember when we first came to live with

Grandma Frannie?" Annabelle asked. "Frannie said Whitehorse wasn't the end of the earth, but it was damned close. She said on a dark night you could see the fires of hell." She laughed but quickly stopped when she saw that she wasn't helping lighten the mood.

"Wait a minute," Chloe said. "This letter was mailed *before* you got here. Whoever sent it knew you were coming here. Either that or figured it would be forwarded to you."

TJ couldn't wrap her head around that. She felt as if someone was always watching her, trying to figure out what she would do next. "How bad is it?" she asked from the kitchen doorway.

Chloe turned to look at her. Annabelle was standing off to the side, hugging herself as if she didn't want to know what the letter said any more than TJ did.

"Read it to me," she said, not wanting to touch it.

Dear Tessa Jane,

I would love to see the expression on your face right now. You really think you can get away from me? I told you, I'm your True Fan until the end. Now that I have your latest book, I hope you won't disappoint me again. I'm not sure I can take any more disappointment from you. I'm not sure what I'll do.

I thought I could help you, make you a better writer. But you've continued to ignore me as if you think I have no value. That hurts me deeply. I'm not sure I can let you go on writing these books.

The only way you can save yourself is if you made up for it in this recent book. Let's both hope that you do.

Still your True Fan until The End

"What is this person talking about?" Chloe asked as she finished reading.

TJ couldn't speak for a moment. The letters had started out being addressed to Ms. St. Clair. Then TJ. Now Tessa Jane. Each growing more familiar.

"TJ, what is it this person wants you to do?" Annabelle asked, worry in her voice.

She sighed. "One of the main characters told a lie but went unpunished."

"So punish the character," Annabelle said. "It's got to be more than that."

"True Fan also wants the lead character to fall for—"

"Durango," Chloe said with a curse.

She looked at her sister. "You read my books?" This day was just filled with surprises.

"Guilty. I hate to ask since it's going to spoil your latest book for me, but Constance doesn't end up with Durango?"

TJ shook her head. "Durango dies in this book."

SILAS HAD WOOD to chop and bring into the cabin. On the way home from town he'd heard that another storm was coming in. He'd bought groceries before leaving Whitehorse since he could be snowed in for a few days with the blizzard that was reportedly coming. As long as he had plenty of firewood, he would be fine.

But when he'd reached home, the one thing he wanted to do more than anything else was start TJ's book. Her books aside, he now couldn't get the woman herself off his mind. When he'd looked into those amazing sea green eyes… He'd started to ask her out even though it was clear that he made her nervous. But just the thought of having a chance to talk to her about books, writing… Not that he hadn't noticed how attractive she was. He shook himself. He had wood to chop.

After unloading everything from town, he made short work of getting enough wood in for the next few days. The first few snowflakes drifted down as he started to carry in the last load of split logs. He stopped for a moment to look up at the heavens. Snowflakes whirled down from a white, low sky. The air was cold and crisp and smelled of the tall pines that surrounded him and his cabin.

But it was the utter silence that captivated him. He'd never known such quiet after living in the city all his life except for his stint in the army overseas. His close friends thought he was crazy for coming here.

"Why the middle of nowhere in Montana?" one friend had asked.

"It's because of that writer he likes," another friend joked. "TJ St. Clair. How'd this guy talk you into something so crazy?"

Silas had let his friends think that the books were written by a man. He'd thought so himself at first, so why not? "I liked the way the writer described the area. It's exactly like in the books."

"Just be glad he's not doing this because of some woman," his friend said.

"That's the worst," the other agreed. "We'd know for sure that he's lost his mind."

They'd all laughed, Silas the heartiest.

TJ MET THE reporter at the Great Northern. She'd suggested it because she knew they would be able to find a quiet corner in the dining room to talk. After ordering coffee, the reporter began to ask her questions.

She'd done dozens of interviews since publishing her first book. Reporters asked many of the same questions. Where do you get your ideas? Everywhere. She'd spent years being a wallflower and watching people. She was fascinated by what made each one tick. The good, the bad, the truly ugly all made for great characters.

What inspired you to write this book? She'd seen a news story on television and while her story had taken a different twist, it had been the starting point.

TJ answered one question after another, adding examples and little asides, all the time her mind on the mountain man, Silas Walker.

Finally the reporter asked her what she knew now that she wished she'd known when she started. How hard it is.

"This is the hardest work I've ever done," TJ said truthfully. "It isn't an eight-to-five job where you go home at night and forget it until the next day. There's no Thank God It's Friday. No paid vacation and sick leave. Once I start a book, those characters are with me until I finish their story. They wake me up in the middle of the night. They nag me until I finish the book."

"So one of the fallacies is that you have all this time on your hands because you don't have to punch a time clock," the reporter said.

TJ laughed and nodded. "Everyone dreams

of staying home, working in their pajamas, not having a boss looking over your shoulder. It's a little more complicated than that. It's a lot of long hours at a computer."

She was glad when the interview was over and she could walk back to the house where her sisters were eagerly waiting. By then, snow had begun to fall. The flakes were huge and drifted on the breeze.

"Did you know it was supposed to snow?" Chloe asked later as Annabelle slowed the SUV to make the turn at the tiny town of Zortman stuck in the side of the Little Rockies. Zortman had a bar-café, post office, church and a small building used as a jail.

Huge flakes drifted down from the dull white sky to stick on the windshield. The SUV's wipers were having a hard time keeping up. Several inches of snow had already fallen on the road. Their tracks were the only ones so far on the road south.

TJ could see patches of dark green through the falling snow as they approached the Little Rockies. The mountains rose from the prairie in steep rock cliffs and pine-covered slopes.

Before the town of Zortman, set back against the cliffs, Annabelle turned off on a road that passed the cemetery and some summer camp-sites. As the road climbed deeper into the mountains, the snow seemed to fall harder.

They had gotten bundled up, determined to get rid of the pall that had fallen over them after the latest letter from True Fan. Annabelle had thrown the ax into the back of the SUV along with some rope to tie the tree on the top—once they found it.

"I'll park up here and then we can get out and walk," Annabelle announced. "I'm sure we'll find the perfect tree."

Chloe groaned as she looked out the window. "I know it's beautiful, but I don't like this. What if we get stuck?"

"It's not that far of a walk into Zortman," Annabelle said as she kept driving up the narrow, snowy road through the dense pines. "Also there are cabins up here. I'm sure we can find someone to help us."

Chloe made a skeptical sound and turned up the radio as a Christmas song came on. She began to sing along, with Annabelle joining in. TJ didn't feel like singing. She'd seen a newer mailbox back on the county road. S. Walker. Silas Walker's cabin must be up this way.

She hadn't wanted to worry her sisters, but there was something about the man. So much so that she had to know if he was True Fan. This latest letter made her even more suspicious that it had to be him. The postmark on the letter had been Whitehorse.

"So True Fan knows someone in all these places where the letters have been mailed," Chloe had said back at the house before they'd left. "She or he gets friends to mail them, saying it's a game she/he is playing with you."

"You're saying True Fan knows someone in Whitehorse who mailed the letter?" Annabelle had said. "But wouldn't that person know TJ?"

"Not necessarily," Chloe had said, and had shot her sister a look.

"Stop trying to make me feel better," TJ had said. The owner of the gift shop had called her Tessa Jane, the name everyone in Whitehorse had known her by. And now her True Fan was also calling her by that name after meeting her at the book signing? Or had True Fan known her real name all along since it was right at the front of the book under copyright?

She knew he could have found out her name in any number of places, but that True Fan was now using it…

Annabelle pulled out in a wide spot and cut the engine and radio. The silence was as deep as the snow around them. "Ready?"

They tugged on coats, snow-pants, boots, hats and mittens and disembarked with Annabelle toting the ax. At first they walked up the road but quickly realized they would have to separate and go into the woods to find a tree.

"Remember no taller than eight feet," Annabelle warned them. "Trees always look smaller out here."

"You'd think she'd been doing this her whole life," Chloe commented to TJ before they split up. "One trip to get a tree with Dawson and now she's an expert." Growing up, their grandmother had had a fake tree, one of the first ones they'd come out with.

TJ stepped off the road into the trees and then waited until her sisters disappeared into the woods before she dropped back down on the snow-covered dirt road. She could see older tire tracks now filling with snow from where someone had driven in here earlier. She followed the tire tracks in the deep snow, determined to find Silas Walker's cabin.

Walking through the falling snow had a dizzying effect on her after a while. It was like being inside a snow globe. She stopped to look back and saw how quickly her tracks were filling in.

TJ had no idea how far she'd gone when she noticed fresh tracks had turned up an even more narrow snowy road that led up the mountain. There were no new tire tracks on the road she'd been following. If Silas Walker had driven back in to his cabin after the signing then there was a good chance these tracks were his.

She decided to follow the tracks in the hope of coming across his cabin. Following the tire tracks, she hadn't gone far when she caught the smell of wood smoke on the air. She kept going through the falling snow, losing track of time and distance.

After continuing to climb up the road deeper into the mountains, she stopped to catch her breath and considered turning back. But she'd gone too far to do that. She told herself that if she didn't come across the cabin soon, she would.

She wasn't worried, but when she looked back, she saw that her boot tracks had filled in. All around her was nothing but white. The snowflakes were falling much harder now. She could barely see the road ahead through the snow. She felt a chill and realized how crazy this had been.

Just a little farther, she told herself, and was almost ready to give up when she spotted smoke rising up out of the trees in the distance. Hurrying now, she headed toward it. Annabelle had said that there were several cabins up here. She told herself that this one had be Silas Walker's. There'd only been one set of tracks this far into the mountains and most of the cabins up here only were used in the summer.

As she drew closer, she saw the truck he'd been driving parked next to the small log cabin. Wet and cold, she hesitated. She knew she should get back to her sisters. They would be worried about her.

From the side of the cabin Silas Walker stepped out carrying a huge armload of firewood, startling her. As if sensing her, he looked up. Surprise registered on his face, then another emotion.

TJ spun around and tried to run back the way she'd come. Her boots slipped on the icy road beneath the snow. She went down hard. Her left leg twisted under her as her boot heel caught on the ice. She let out a cry of pain. Struggling to get up in the deep snow, she realized her ankle was hurt badly. She dropped back to the ground, grimacing in pain, suddenly terrified because she wasn't going far on this ankle.

When she was suddenly lifted off the ground, she screamed. She struggled, but Silas had her in a bear hug and this man was way too large and strong for her to overpower him. Her scream was suddenly cut off by a large gloved hand over her mouth.

"Stop struggling, you're only going to hurt yourself worse," he said next to her ear. "I'm going to set you down on your good leg. Okay?"

She sucked in air through her nose and stopped fighting him to nod.

The moment he set her down, she slugged him in the stomach. It was like hitting a block wall and turning, she tried to run and immediately collapsed on her bad ankle.

He was on her again, covering her mouth as she began screaming in both pain and terror. "One of us is crazy. Since it's not me," he said, "we're taking this inside the cabin where it's warm." He tossed her over one broad shoulder and turned them both toward the cabin.

She screamed and pounded his back, but it had no effect as he strode up the porch steps of the cabin, shoved open the door and stepped inside. Swinging her off his shoulder, he dropped her unceremoniously into a large overstuffed chair.

Immediately she tried to get up, letting out a cry as she put pressure on her hurt ankle. Not that she was going anywhere even if she hadn't twisted it. He dropped a hand to her shoulder and held her in place as he kicked the door shut. It was warm inside the cabin and at the smell of something cooking her stomach growled, although she hardly noticed.

"What are you doing out in a blizzard?" he demanded, towering over her. He smelled of freshly cut pine. There was a maleness about him that was intimidating and at the same time intoxicating, even if he was her demented True

Fan. She thought of a mountain lion on the prowl and felt like a small rabbit wanting to run for its life.

"You have to let me go!"

He held up his hands. "Not until you tell me what's going on. What are you doing here, TJ?"

So he had recognized her, even bundled up with her hat covering half of her face.

"I was out looking for a Christmas tree. I got turned around." She started to push out of the chair but he held up his hand.

"Hold on. Looking for a Christmas tree? And you just happened to stumble onto my cabin? Tell me you didn't come up here by yourself."

"I didn't. I came with my sisters. They'll be looking for me. That's why I have to go. They'll be worried."

But even as she said it, she knew they wouldn't be able to find her. They thought she'd come up here to find a Christmas tree. They would be looking for her closer to where Annabelle had parked the SUV. By now they could have a tree and be loading it.

She imagined them calling her name, joking around until they started to get worried when she hadn't appeared. Would they try to track her? As hard as it was snowing right now, her tracks would have filled in. They'd never be able to find her.

What had she been thinking? She hadn't. She'd acted on instinct and this is where it had led her.

She tried to get up again. He didn't push her back down, but he did move to crouch down in front of her. "TJ, you're a terrible liar, no offense. What are you really doing here?"

If only she knew. It wasn't as if she'd had a plan. She'd wanted to find his cabin. She'd wanted to spy on him. She'd wanted to learn more about him because she believed he was

True Fan? Or because of that exhilbarating and yet confusing mixture of strong feelings she'd had the first time she'd laid eyes on him?

What she hadn't wanted to do was get caught and end up trapped in his cabin with him. It galled her what she'd done, since there was no way she would have let the heroine in her books do something this stupid.

Past him, she could see just how small the cabin was. It was only one room with a fireplace, a very small kitchen area, the chair she was sitting in and a bed. Next to the bed was a makeshift desk. It was what she saw on it that stopped her heart.

Sitting on the desk was a large old manual typewriter.

Chapter Nine

TJ felt her eyes widen in alarm. Silas had seen her look in the direction of the typewriter. Now he was frowning at her in a way that turned her blood to slush.

She thought of all the books she'd written where the heroine escaped by hitting the villain with a makeshift weapon. Or catching him off guard and kicking him in his private parts before bolting for the door.

While there was a floor lamp next to the chair, she couldn't imagine how she could grab it, swing it and hit him hard enough to get away. That was if she could walk on her ankle—let alone run.

But given no other option—she sat up a little. He was crouched directly in front of her. She'd barely kicked out with her good leg when he grabbed it, stopping her foot before it could reach its mark.

"That only works in your books," he said, his voice deep and rough. "Most of the time, it only makes the bad guy more angry. Let's quit playing around. Tell me what's going on."

"I know who you are." She hated that she sounded near tears. "You're my True Fan."

He frowned again. "Yes, I'm a fan of your books but…"

She felt fear give away to anger. "You've been sending me the letters!"

"Letters?" he repeated.

"Don't deny it. I know it was you who pushed me in front of the truck in New York yesterday morning."

He rocked back on his haunches. "Whoa. Yes, I was there, luckily for you. I didn't realize that you even saw me. Only I didn't push you," he said, enunciating each word. "I was the one who *saved* you before you became roadkill."

"Right, you just *happened* to be walking past."

"No, as a matter of fact, I was following someone." He made a face as if he saw what she was thinking. "It wasn't *you*. I was on a stakeout."

"I know you're not a cop anymore because you got fired."

"Did some research on me, did you?" He grinned. "I'm flattered. But don't believe everything you read in the paper. Anyway, I work for a private investigative business now. Or I did. I just took a leave of absence. Or did you already know that as well? And, sorry, but I haven't been writing you any letters."

"You've been taunting me for months. Admit it. I just got your latest threatening letter today."

"You've got the wrong guy."

"Really? Next you're going to tell me that you just happen to have a manual typewriter like the letters have all been written on," she said, jabbing a finger in its direction. She saw his sheepish look. "That's what I thought."

"You have it all wrong," he said, getting to his feet. "If you must know, I've been trying to write a book." He shrugged, looking embarrassed. "I use a manual up here because the power goes out more than it's on this time of year. I read that you write every day so I've been trying to do that." He moved to the woodstove. "You inspired me to at least try. Unfortunately, I don't have your talent."

She watched him throw another log into the woodstove. Did he really think she believed

him? "I need to go. My sisters will be looking for me."

He turned to look at her. "Have you checked
out the weather outside?"

She hadn't, but she did so now. The wind had
picked up, whirling snow in a blinding white
that covered everything. Worse, the visibility
was only a few yards. She'd grown up in this
county. She knew how easy it was to get lost.
Ranchers often tied a rope from the house to
the barn so they didn't wander off track and
freeze to death.

"Once the storm stops, I can try to get us
out of here in my pickup," he was saying. "But
the truth is, I barely made it back earlier with
a load of wood I cut from that beetle kill area
by the road. I shouldn't have to tell you how
slick that road into the cabin is. By the way,
how is your ankle?"

"It's fine." She started to get up. He didn't
move to stop her. But as she put pressure on

her twisted ankle, she winced in pain. Who was she kidding? She wasn't going anywhere on that leg even if she could find her way back. She dropped into the chair and dug out her cell phone.

"Good luck with that," he said as he watched her. "I've never been able to get much coverage in a storm. Sometimes a text will go through."

TJ saw that he was right. She only had two bars. She bit her lower lip, fighting back tears as her call didn't go through. Her sisters would be frantic.

She sent a text. At Walker's cabin until storm lets up. It was the best she could do since the text appeared to have gone through.

Raising her gaze, she realized that at least Annabelle and Chloe were together. While she was the one in real trouble.

"LOOK, MAYBE WE could start over," Silas said, seeing how upset she was. "We're stuck here until the storm stops. By then, your sisters will have Search and Rescue looking for you. In the meantime, I've got some beef stew and some homemade bread I baked in the wood-stove yesterday. It was my first attempt so I'm not making any promises."

She swallowed and looked out at the storm before turning back to him.

"Are you all right?" he asked quietly.

"I shouldn't have come here."

No, she shouldn't have. "Hey, you thought I was this person who's been writing you threatening letters. Actually, I'm relieved. I couldn't understand your reaction to me at the gift shop or at your signing. I didn't think I was that scary." Still she said nothing. "You really think someone pushed you yesterday in New York."

"I know someone did. I was shoved in front of that truck."

She was looking at him as if she wasn't convinced it hadn't been him. He could see now where she might have gotten that idea. He should have stuck around and talked to her. But he would have lost the person he was tailing. As it was, he did anyway.

"That was pretty gutsy of you to come looking for me the way you did. Given you thought I was the person who was writing you threatening letters let alone suspecting I pushed you in front of a truck. Probably not your best plan. Good thing I'm not that person."

"Good thing," she said, a little sarcastically. "Otherwise I would be trapped here with someone who wants to hurt me."

He rubbed his whiskered jaw. "How can I prove to you that I'm not this fan you say has been taunting you?" He stepped over to the typewriter. "Truth is, I admire the devil out of you. You're why I wanted to write my own book. I thought it would be easy." He laughed, picked up a handful of typewritten pages and came back over to where she was sitting.

To his surprise, she seemed to flinch at the sight of the paper. "Don't worry, I wasn't going to ask you to read it." He realized that she was staring at the paper as if…as if what?

She snatched a sheet from his hand. "Where did you get this?" she said, holding up the paper. His expression must have conveyed his total confusion. "Copy paper is usually white or some color. This is discolored. There even appear to be watermarks on some of it as if—"

"As if it was stored in a basement for years?" he asked. "I bought it at a garage sale in town last summer."

"*Whose* garage sale?" She sounded as if she didn't believe him. But then again, she hadn't believed anything he'd said.

"How should I know whose garage sale? Remember? I'm new here." He could see that she was still expecting more of an answer. "It was some elderly woman. Her house was for sale. Apparently she'd had boxes of the stuff in her basement for a while. She was practically giving it away."

"Why would she have boxes of it in her basement?"

"I have no idea. Wait. I might have overheard someone say she used to have a business in town that sold office products. Is it really that important to you? I bought one of the boxes filled with reams of paper. You're welcome to—"

"The person who has been sending me the threatening letters typed them on a manual typewriter like the one you have on paper exactly like this." She held up the sheet, her eyes glittering with tears. "Still going to tell me that you aren't True Fan?"

SILAS HELD UP both hands. "Maybe, since we have a little time now that we're snowed in, I can convince you of my innocence. In the meantime, why don't you get out of those wet outer clothes?" he suggested. "By the way, if you have to use the facilities, there's only an outhouse in the back. It's a short walk, but if you can't make it out there with your ankle, I'll be happy to help you."

TJ wished he hadn't mentioned it because now she felt the need to go. She pushed to her feet, grimacing as she put weight on her ankle. Silas was at her side in two long strides.

"Lean on me," he suggested as he walked her to the back door off the kitchen. As he opened the door, a gust of wind showered them both with snow crystals. They stepped out into winter, Silas closing the door behind them.

He was right. It was a short walk and he'd shoveled earlier. But the snow had filled in the path. Tucking their heads into their coats they made their way to the outhouse.

"Sorry. It's pretty primitive. No hurry," he said as he opened the door and let her limp inside. "I'll wait at the back door of the cabin. I'll come help when I see you."

She closed the door. It was freezing in the one-hole outhouse. She couldn't remember the last time she'd used one. Drawing down her pants was no easy job as bundled up as she was. As she lowered herself to the wood seat she was sure her behind would freeze to it.

No hurry, Silas had said, but she hurried, anxious to get her pants pulled back up to get heat to return to her backside. Shivering, she opened the outhouse door. Good to his word, he came charging out.

As they made their way to the back door of the cabin, TJ saw that the storm had only worsened. She thought of her sisters and felt horrible for taking off the way she had. She just hoped they were smart enough not to be out looking for her in this. Hopefully Chloe had gotten the message she'd sent.

Back inside, Silas led her to the sink and provided her with soap and warm water that he'd heated on the woodstove in a large kettle. She washed her hands, dried them on the towel he handed her and let him lead her over to the chair again. While he busied himself at the stove, she got out of her wet boots, coat and ski pants. Down to a sweater and jeans and socks, she shivered in the chair until Silas brought her over a quilt to wrap up in. She watched him take her wet things and hang them up on hooks by the door, telling herself he had to be True Fan, and yet…

As she watched him, she told herself that a man who was this thoughtful couldn't possibly have written those vile things about her. But like her other readers, he probably thought he knew her, thought he knew what was best for her.

The man unsettled her no matter who he was. She reconciled that strange feeling she'd had at the gift shop when their gazes had met.

She'd seen…darkness. Something dangerous. Something violent. She tried to shake off the memory. Where had those feelings come from? Worse, because she still felt them, why were they so strong?

She tried not to flinch as Silas pulled up a stool that had been by the fire and sat down in front of her, his expression somber. "How serious were these threats against you?"

TJ debated how much to tell him. If he was True Fan, then he already knew, so what was his game? And if he wasn't? "One of them suggested I should kill myself and do the reading world a favor. Another said I should die like one of my villains in my books. The latest one just indicated that the letter writer couldn't let me keep writing these books, that this would have to end."

He shook his head. "How did this all get started?"

"Why the interest?"

He smiled. "Believe it or not, I'm still a law-man at heart. I like catching the bad guys. But I also admire you and enjoy your books. Since we're going to be here until the storm passes... Maybe I can be of assistance."

TJ couldn't help being skeptical. It came with her personality. Maybe that was why she wrote what she did. She didn't trust what was behind a smile or kind words. Grandma Frannie used to tell her to lighten up. Like that was possible.

More to the point, she wasn't sure what to make of Silas Walker. All the evidence pointed to him being True Fan. So was this just him still taunting her?

Looking into his blue eyes, she thought she saw genuine concern. She felt confused, thrown off balance by the man. She remembered how easily he had thrown her over his shoulder and carried her into the house. If he was True Fan...

"It started like any other letter from a fan,"

she told him, gauging his expression as she talked. She told him about the first few letters from the person who called him or herself True Fan's being complimentary, all the time studying his face, looking for...looking for a lie in all that blue. But she saw nothing but sympathy and a growing anger at True Fan.

When she finished he got up from the stool without a word and moved to the woodstove. He seemed to be thinking as he stirred the stew.

She studied his broad back, wondering why he'd been fired from the police department. "Well?" she prodded.

He stirred the stew for a minute or two before he turned back to her. "If you really were purposely pushed into the traffic yesterday, then we would have to assume your True Fan either lived in New York or just happened to be there yesterday. But if you're right about the paper True Fan is using to write the letters on coming from the same place as I got mine, then…"

She nodded, her heart pounding. Was this where he told her it had been him all along? "True Fan had to have gone to the same garage sale you did. Someone with connections to both New York City and Whitehorse since True Fan also took a photograph of my apartment," she reminded him.

He raised his gaze to hers. "A fan anywhere in the country could have had a friend in New York snap a photo of your apartment. Also, your near accident yesterday could have been just that. I think your True Fan is right here in Montana."

"Right where you just happened to be. Right where you just happened to be passing by yesterday."

He mugged a face at her. "The reason it's called a coincidence is because they do exist. I had no idea the woman I grabbed to keep her from falling in front of a delivery truck yesterday was you." He crossed his heart with the index finger of his left hand.

"You're left-handed." The words were out before she could stop them.

He looked confused again for a moment before he smiled. "I forgot. Your heroine Constance Ryan always falls for left-handed men. I'm betting there were a couple of left-handed boyfriends in your past." He turned back to the stove.

He'd be wrong about that. There had been one though—Marc. He'd been left-handed and one of the mistakes she'd made when she'd first started writing was that she'd made her heroine in her ongoing series too much like herself. *Write what you know*, she'd always been told. She didn't know anyone as well as she knew herself.

But while Constance Ryan always fell for left-handed men, she was the woman TJ wished she was. Unfortunately the similarities were obvious to anyone who knew her. Constance was a blonde with aquamarine-blue eyes, five foot six, curvy. A woman who loved spicy food and drank her coffee black and by the gallon.

But that was where the similarities stopped. Constance was daring. As a private investigator, she took on cases that others had turned down. She was smart and determined. Even after almost getting killed in every book, she still came back for more.

Constance also loved men—and men loved her. She always ended up curled up in bed with some handsome man. She wasn't one to stay long with any of them. Constance Ryan lived her life the way TJ wished she could.

But TJ was too much of a prude who'd hardly dated, even at college. Also she believed in happy-ever-after—even if her alter ego didn't. She didn't want a string of men.

She just wanted that one man who would make her heart pound.

Like this man was doing right now. Only was it fear? Or something just as dangerous, given the two of them were alone, snowed-in deep in the mountains?

"I CAN SEE why you thought I was writing the threatening letters to you," Silas said after dishing them both up bowls of hot beef stew with a side of his homemade bread slathered in butter.

He'd pushed his stool over against the wall and leaned against it as he ate. He was glad to see that TJ seemed to have relaxed a little. Outside, the blizzard was still raging. He'd built the cabin to withstand the winter cold so it was cozy inside, but he could hear the wind and see snow piling up at the windows. He wondered if the snow would be too deep to drive out once the storm stopped.

"I've been thinking how to go about finding this fan of yours," he said between bites. Because he'd realized he had to help her whether she wanted it or not. The only way to prove to her that he wasn't True Fan was to find the culprit. Also, finding the nasty letter writer with TJ definitely had its appeal. He'd never dreamed he would get a chance to even have a cup of coffee with her—let alone spend time in his cabin with her.

"I can't wait to hear your plan." She'd stopped, her spoon in midair, to look at him. He could see she was still suspicious. He didn't blame her. Given the evidence against him, he would have thought the same thing she did.

"It seems simple to me. It all comes down to the old discolored copy paper. Anyone can shoot a photograph of the outside of your apartment—"

"How would they know where I lived unless they had contacts…say, inside the police department?"

He smiled at that as he watched her take a bite of the stew. He could see that she liked it, which made him a lot happier than it should have. Pride cometh before the fall, his father used to say. "You like the bread?"

"You really baked this in that woodstove?" she asked skeptically.

"I did. See that iron box on the top? It's an oven. This is my first attempt. I'll get better."

"It's very good. I've never attempted bread—even in a real oven."

He smiled, warmed by her compliment more than by the stew. He took a couple more bites before he said, "As to the question of how to find out where you lived…all anyone had to do was follow you home from a book signing. How many have you done in New York and gone straight home afterward?"

She didn't answer, his point taken.

"As for the push, there were so many people rushing around with Christmas shopping. I got jostled myself just moments before that. I didn't see anyone push you but I was in a tight crowd of people who were forced to the curb. I just caught you falling out of the corner of my eye, but there were people in front of me, including a woman with a huge shopping bag who could have hit you."

He watched her lick her lips after taking a bite of the bread covered with real butter. No butter substitute in his kitchen, ever. He could tell she was considering his theory.

"So let's say True Fan knows someone in New York who could have followed me from a book signing and taken a photo of my apartment from the street."

"Or she could have even hired someone to do it," he added, thinking about the private investigative business he'd been working for since leaving the police department. It was amazing to him what people would pay to learn.

TJ nodded, no doubt thinking of Constance, the heroine in her books. "So then it would just come down to the copy paper you both purchased at a garage sale last summer in Whitehorse?"

"August. I also bought this stool there."

Her gaze darkened to deep sea green. "So it's someone who lives in Whitehorse." She shivered and for the first time, he thought she might actually be considering that it wasn't him.

"I'd suspect it's someone who knows you and has reason to be jealous of your success," he said. "Maybe an old rival? An old boyfriend? Maybe even a former friend."

Chapter Ten

"I still can't believe you really made this bread," TJ said as she accepted another piece. Her walk to find his cabin had left her famished.

He grinned, obviously pleased. "For my first time, I think I got lucky, huh."

"It's delicious and so is the stew," TJ said, feeling conflicted. Could she trust this man? Sometimes the way he looked at her with those potent blue eyes, it made her squirm uncomfortably. It was when she glimpsed a dangerous edge to him that she had her doubts. She tried not to think about the predicament she was in—trapped in a cabin in a blizzard in the mountains with a man she didn't trust.

Common sense told her he had to be True Fan.

But after seven books, she knew from experience that the villain often proved to be the person you least expected—not the obvious one. Of course, that was fiction and this felt more like any real life she'd lived so far.

There was something so charming about Silas because of his easygoing manner. And that he was a little domesticated made him even more appealing. He seemed almost shy around her. She saw none of the anger that had practically dripped from True Fan's threatening letters.

After months of running scared she wasn't sure she could trust her instincts, though. Look where they'd brought her.

As she finished her stew and bread she noticed it had gotten dark, although it was hard to tell how late it was since the thick-falling snow still made it fairly light out. She pulled out her phone, hoping for a response from one of her sisters, but there was nothing. She looked at the time and realized with a start that she would be spending the night in this cabin with this man. Her heart began to pound a little harder.

Silas rose to his feet, stepping to her to take her bowl and spoon. "Don't worry," he said as if reading her mind. "You can have the bed when you get tired. I have a sleeping bag I'll drag out. I've curled up in front of the fire on the rug more times than I can remember when I was building this place. The bed came later."

He moved to the makeshift kitchen. Earlier, he'd refilled the kettle on the stove. Now she watched him wash up their dishes in a pan in the sink. He was so self-sufficient. Handsome too in a rough, untamed way that both intrigued her and scared her.

"Don't you get lonely out here?" she asked, wondering if there was a woman in his life back in New York.

"Just the opposite," he said without turning around. "I come here for the peace and quiet. Listen." He stopped what he was doing to half turn to look at her.

She heard nothing but the pop and hiss of the fire in the woodstove.

"Not one siren to be heard. No traffic. No honking taxis. No loud music from the apartment next door." He let out a sigh. "This is why I love this place. Sometimes I just have to get away from all the racket. Here I get up when I feel like it, I go to bed when I'm tired. I spend my days working on the cabin, cutting wood for the stove, cooking my own meals. When I'm not working, I'm reading. Or attempting to write," he said with a chuckle as he went back to his dishes.

"I had forgotten what it was like living in Montana," TJ had to admit.

"That's right, you grew up in Whitehorse."

She nodded, remembering sledding and ice-skating in the winter, tubing the river in the summer. She'd forgotten what small-town living was like, the slower pace, the unlimited space, the quiet. "I hadn't realized that I missed it."

He turned then to look at her as he dried his big hands on a dish towel. "You must enjoy the glamour and excitement of New York City though. Isn't that why you live there? You can write anywhere."

"I did enjoy the city, especially at first. It felt as if it was where I needed to be to have the career I wanted."

"But now?"

She shook her head. "I hate it. True Fan has ruined the city for me. I don't feel safe there anymore." She let out a bitter laugh. "I don't feel safe anywhere."

He put down the dish towel carefully and turned to lean back against the kitchen counter. "I'm so sorry about that. It's another reason we have to find this person and put a stop to it. I would imagine it's also been hard for you to write."

She looked away. "You have no idea. Or maybe you do."

Silas cocked his head. "I know you still don't trust that I'm not this person. That's okay. You have to be skeptical to write the books you do—and to be safe. But I promise you I'm going to find True Fan even if you don't want to help me." He pushed off the counter. "Hot chocolate or tea?"

"Tea."

TJ watched him put a smaller kettle on the stove and prepare two cups with tea bags. "I'd like to read some of your book."

He froze for a moment before turning. "You're going to laugh, but right now I'm more terrified than when I'm facing down a junkie with a gun."

"If you don't want me to…"

"Oh, that's just it. The thought of you reading anything I've written both excites and terrifies me. Didn't you feel that way?"

She smiled, nodding. "I remember the first time I took a writing class. I just wanted the instructor to tell me I could do this."

"Did the instructor?"

"No. Looking back, the woman didn't know anything more than I did about how to have a writing career, even though she'd sold a couple of books. I don't think she wanted to get my hopes up since by then she knew how hard it was."

"Well, you don't have to worry about that with me. I enjoy writing, so I'll keep at it hoping I get better no matter what you say. But I really would appreciate your opinion."

Crossing to the typewriter, he reached beside it and picked up a few pages.

"Give me the first chapter," she said. Aspiring writers always wanted to show her their favorite chapter in the middle, not realizing an editor would never read that chapter if they couldn't get past the first one.

He brought over a dozen sheets of paper. She noticed the way he held them in those large hands, like he was carrying a bird with a broken wing.

"You don't have to read the whole chapter," he said, carefully handing her the pages.

The first thing she noticed was that the pages had been typed with a new ribbon. There were none of the light and dark letters like on True Fan's.

Silas stood over her for a moment, then quickly moved away to take his coat from the hook by the door. "I'm going to bring more wood in from the porch," he said. "I suspect the temperature is going to drop tonight. I'll have to keep the stove going." With that, he went out the door on a gust of cold, snowy wind.

For a moment, TJ watched the snowflakes that had swept in melt on the wood floor. Then she turned to the pages of his book and began to read.

SILAS STOOD OUT on the porch in the blizzard smiling like a fool. TJ St. Clair was reading his book. He felt his stomach roil. What if it stunk as badly as he feared it did? What if she told him to use it to start his next woodstove fire? Or maybe worse, he thought, what if she told him it wasn't bad? That it was good enough that he should keep at it? That he had promise?

He wasn't sure which was his greatest fear—fear of failure or of success. They scared him in ways his job never had—even when he'd recently been shot. He rubbed his thigh unconsciously, realizing that his limp had been hardly noticeable. Or maybe he'd tried harder for it not to show around TJ.

Silas felt a shudder when he thought of her True Fan. How dangerous was this person? Would they really go through with their threats if pushed too far? More than ever, he was determined to find the person and put an end to all this.

The wind whipped snow into his face and down his neck. He shivered and hurriedly grabbed an armload of split firewood to take back inside. By now, TJ would have read far enough that she'd have an opinion. Feeling as if he was about to step in front of a firing squad, he told himself he could take whatever she had to offer, and pushed open the door to the cabin.

At first he didn't see her. The chair was

empty and for one heart-stopping moment, he thought she had taken off out the back door. But as his gaze shifted, he saw her standing on one foot by the woodstove. She had the small kettle handle in one hand and was pouring boiling water in each of his mismatched mugs.

He dropped the load of wood in the bin near the stove and tried to slow his pulse. "You shouldn't be on your ankle."

"I hopped over. The kettle was boiling." She studied him. "You thought I'd left."

"I thought I was going to have to try to find you out in that storm. I wasn't looking forward to it."

She nodded. "That's the only reason?"

"Maybe I like your company." He could tell that wasn't what she meant at all. She thought he'd lured her here and that he was never going to let her leave. "Here, let me finish the tea." He helped her over to the chair and she dropped into it. "Are you warm enough?"

She nodded and seemed to watch him as he went back to the stove, returning with her cup of tea.

"I'd ask if you want sugar…"

"Constance Ryan takes sugar in her coffee, not me," she said, taking the mug of tea. "We aren't our characters."

"Aren't we? I knew you took your coffee black. Wasn't sure about tea." He thought of his own protagonist in the book he'd started. It was him and it wasn't. But still there was so much of him in his words that he felt vulnerable, something he'd seldom felt even on duty as a cop.

TJ sipped her tea as he hung up his coat and walked back to the counter to pick up his mug.

"I hate to even ask," he said, seeing his chapter lying on the footstool near the chair. He couldn't tell if she'd read any of it, let alone the whole chapter.

TJ NOTICED THE way the large mug disappeared in his hands. Silas seemed so gentle and yet she'd seen the way his muscles had bulged when he'd carried in the wood. For a man his size, he moved with a grace that again reminded her of a mountain lion.

"You have talent, but I don't have to tell you that," she said as she picked up the chapter from the stool and he moved to it to sit down. "I was drawn right into your story. I wanted to read more." He was eyeing her as if he was waiting for a "but." "You've had other people read some of your book, right? I'm sure they've told you…"

He shook his head. "You're the first and only."

She couldn't help being surprised. "Then you really didn't know."

"I'm trying to decide if you're just being nice."

"I'm not. The one thing I learned a long time

ago was that people who tell you you're better than you are are of no help. You need real criticism if you're going to get better, and I believe we have to continue to strive to do so."

He seemed to let out a breath before taking a sip of his tea. "Like I said, I enjoy writing so I'll keep going, but I'm overjoyed to hear it's okay."

"It's more than okay," she said. "I won't promise you that you can have a career writing. Just being good isn't enough. It takes determination and some luck."

"I have the determination. I'm not so sure about the luck." He smiled. "But I feel lucky right now. It's nice to have company."

They drank their tea in the comfort of the cabin as the storm raged on outside. The stove popped and crackled. Silas got up to throw more wood on the fire, then turned and looked at her shyly. "You wouldn't be interested in playing some cards, would you?"

She laughed. "What did you have in mind?"

"I don't even care. Crazy eights. Old maid. Five-card stud. I love to play cards and I'm sick of solitaire."

"My sisters and I used to play all the time. Do people still play with actual cards now that they have virtual games?"

"I have no idea," he said as he brought over a deck of worn cards. From a space behind her chair, he pulled out a small folding table. "You can even beat me. That's how desperate I am," he said with a laugh.

TJ snuggled into the chair. She hadn't played cards in years. She watched Silas shuffle the deck and realized she was beginning to trust him. She hoped that wouldn't be her last mistake.

Chapter Eleven

They played cards until after midnight. Silas couldn't recall a time he'd had more fun. TJ was an excellent player no matter what game they played. She challenged him. He couldn't remember the last woman who'd done that. She'd relaxed during their games and he'd gotten to see the woman behind the best seller.

She was fun and funny, sharp-witted. He liked her, and not just because she thought he had talent.

It wasn't until the last game that she began to look nervous again. He put the cards away and went to the built-in drawers on the other side of the bed. Pulling out one of his T-shirts, he held it up.

"I think this will cover everything but your toes if you're interested in wearing it to sleep in," he said. "I'll go out and get some more wood and give you a chance to change. Or you can sleep in your clothes. Whatever you prefer." He put the T-shirt down on the bed. "You need to go out back first?"

She shook her head. They'd made several trips out to the bathroom earlier during their card games.

"Sorry, I don't have a spare toothbrush. Wasn't expecting company, but there is toothpaste and water by the sink. Let me know if there is anything else you need." He headed for his coat by the door.

Once outside, he killed time thinking about True Fan. If it hadn't been for this crazed reader, he might never have gotten this close to TJ. That was a thought he wasn't about to share. He also tried not imagining her in his T-shirt. The thought made him grin and ache at the same time.

It had been so long since he'd been truly interested in a woman. He blamed it on everything that had been going on in his life. But he knew that had only been part of it. He'd missed the companionship. Hell, he'd missed the sex. And just thinking of TJ wearing his T-shirt… He shook off the thought.

If he wanted this to go any further, he'd best take it slow. The woman was beyond skittish. She was running scared. Not just that. She still didn't trust him. He hoped to fix that.

He warned himself that she'd be gone as soon as the storm quit. That's if her sisters didn't show up with the National Guard and probably half the county's lawmen before the night was over. Otherwise, he would get her out of the mountains in the morning one way or another.

The thought that he might not see her again was almost physically painful. He'd been captivated by her since her first book. Now that he'd gotten to spend this time with her, well, he didn't want it to end.

That alone surprised him. He dated in New York, but usually he was fine only seeing a woman a time or two. He didn't feel that way about TJ—even if he hadn't been worried about her.

Loading up another armful of wood, he tapped at the door. Hearing nothing, he stepped in. She was tucked in bed, the down comforter up to her chin. She looked so damned cute in his bed. He quickly closed the door on a blast of snow and wind and, turning his back to her, dumped the wood and took off his coat.

Seeing her in his bed made him ache. It also threw him a little off-balance. He felt both protective and attracted to this woman. Just the thought of kissing her… "Have everything you need?" he asked, his voice sounded strange to his ears.

She nodded and watched him with just her eyes as he went to the area by the bed, opened a cabinet and pulled out his sleeping bag.

Rolling it out on the rug in front of the fire, he turned out the lights and lay down on top of it. A moment later, she tossed him a pillow from the bed.

"Thanks," he said into the quiet darkness. The storm had let up a little. He felt like he did when he was a kid at a sleepover. He didn't want to sleep. He wanted to talk about all the things that interested him, from life on other planets, to Big Foot's possible existence, to what TJ's favorite Christmas gift of all time was.

"Do you remember lying in bed waiting for Santa?" she asked from the darkness.

He chuckled. "I do. I never wanted to close my eyes. I was afraid I'd miss it."

"I hated it when I found out he wasn't real."

"He's not?" The fire crackled and after a few moments, he realized that she'd gone to sleep.

TJ WOKE TO find the cabin empty. The bedroll and pillow were no longer on the floor in front of the woodstove. And while a fire was going, Silas was nowhere to be seen. Sitting up, she saw that the pillow she'd tossed him was lying next to her on the bed. His bedroll had apparently been put away.

Had he only gone to the outhouse and would be back any minute?

She heard something outside. For a moment she thought it was his heavy tread on the porch, but soon realized it was him trying to start his pickup. She threw back the covers and got up. Her ankle was better, only tender to the touch and black and blue along one side.

Silas had been right about his T-shirt. It fell to her ankles. As she slipped it off, she sniffed it as if she thought it might contain his scent. She held it for a moment, feeling like a teenage girl again, before tossing it on the bed and quickly pulling on the clothes she'd worn. She'd moved to the chair and was putting on her socks when she heard him come up the porch stairs and into the cabin.

"Good morning!" he greeted her, brushing snow off his coat and stomping it from his boots before stepping in on the rug. "Truck's cleared off and the motor turned right over after a few tries. If I have to, I can chain up all four tires to get us out of here. I wasn't sure how much of a hurry you're in to get home."

Last night she'd been champing at the bit. This morning, she hated to leave this cabin. Hated to leave Silas. Which was why she needed to, even if she wasn't worried that her sisters would be frantic.

She glanced around the cabin. "I can go

whenever you're ready. I appreciate your taking me back to town."

"Not a problem. I've enjoyed having you here. But I'm not much of a host if I don't offer you breakfast," he said.

She was tempted. The warmth of this cabin, the scent of homemade bread, the good-natured, handsome man standing in the doorway. At that moment, she desperately wanted Silas Walker to be anything but True Fan.

"Thank you, but I really should get back. My sisters will be worried even after the text." Actually, more worried after the text.

He nodded, not looking any more anxious to leave than she was. "I'll be in the pickup. Come out when you're ready." He turned then and disappeared back outside.

TJ stepped to the hooks by the door, pulled down her coat, tugged on her snow-pants and boots. She took one last look around the cabin, thinking she might never see it again. Out of the corner of her eye she saw the typewriter. Curiosity killed the cat and every B movie heroine who decided to see what the noise was in the basement. Still, she moved to the typewriter and shuffled through the papers. Just pages of his book. She checked the trash can next to it. No partial letters written in too much haste.

Silas Walker wasn't True Fan. But Silas wouldn't be living out here in the woods unless he was running from something. She hated that she was thinking like her sister Chloe, the investigative reporter. But something had to explain those glimpses of darkness she'd seen in his blue eyes.

Walking out of the cabin, she limped her way through the deep snow to the pickup, where he was waiting behind the wheel. He leaned over the seat, pushed open the passenger side door and held it for her to get in.

"Shoot, I forgot about your ankle," he said. "I should have offered to help you."

"It's better, but thank you. Are you always so cheerful in the morning?" she asked.

"Do I detect that you aren't?" he asked with a laugh as he shifted the pickup into low gear. "Cross your fingers."

They chugged up the hill, the back of the pickup sliding a few times before they reached the road she'd come down earlier. There was no sign that anyone had been down the road last night.

"Okay," Silas said with a sigh of relief. "That was the worst of it. At least I hope so."

The sun topped the pines, making the fresh snow sparkle so bright that it was blinding. "It's so beautiful," she breathed. "I'd forgotten days like this."

He glanced over at her, but said nothing as he quickly turned back to his driving. The pickup bucked and slid and chugged until they reached an even wider snowy dirt road and finally the plowed, though snow-packed highway.

Silas patted the dash and said, "I knew you could do it, Gertrude."

"Gertrude?" she asked with a laugh. She was relieved they'd gotten out of the mountains without any trouble. She was also relieved that the easiness between them had returned.

"Be careful," Silas joked. "Don't insult her."

"I wouldn't dream of it," TJ said.

"Old Gert here reminds me of Constance."

She lifted a brow as she looked over at him. "Your truck reminds you of the heroine in my books?" She couldn't help feeling a little offended, since she and Constance had a lot in common. No man had ever compared her to a pickup.

"Both Gert and Connie are dependable. They're up for anything when you need them. They both have their own kind of charm."

TJ smiled. "Well, when you put it that way…"

He chuckled and drove, looking comfortable behind the wheel even though the highway was slick and the landscape so white that it was hard to tell where the two-lane began and ended.

Normally, TJ would have been nervous about going off the road and ending up in a snowbank. But there was something about Silas that was a lot like his truck.

Chapter Twelve

"I don't know how to thank you," TJ said when Silas pulled up in front of the house. "It was interesting and…fun."

He grinned. "Glad to hear it. I was delighted for the company. It was nice visiting with you. But I hope we see each other soon." He jumped out to open her door. "I meant what I said about helping find that fan of yours. If I can figure out which house I went to for that garage sale and what happened to the woman who sold me the paper, do you want to go with me to talk to her?"

She couldn't help her smile. "I do."

He nodded, his smile broadening. "Then I'll let you know."

"Thank you." She gave him a nod and a wave as she started for the house. She heard him close her door, go around and climb behind the wheel. As he pulled away behind her, she hoped she wasn't wrong about the man. His words had made her all warm inside. Not to mention what happened when she'd looked into those blue eyes.

He was the kind of man a woman could fall hard for. Which made her all the more leery. There was a reason Constance never gave away her heart in the books. Her creator had given her heart away once, only to have it broken badly. To say they were both gun-shy was to put it mildly.

She'd barely reached the porch when her sisters came rushing out, both talking at once.

As Silas drove away, a sheriff's patrol car

pulled up out front. TJ and her sisters turned to see Sheriff McCall Crawford climb out.

"Are you all right?" Annabelle whispered.

"I'm fine. What is the sheriff doing here?" she whispered back.

"Chloe called her."

Of course she did. TJ sighed under her breath. "Did you get a tree?"

Annabelle smiled. "Of course. We're putting it up later."

The three waited until Sheriff Crawford joined them before going inside. Chloe, who clearly had taken charge, ushered them all into the kitchen.

"I see you made it home safe and sound," the sheriff said to TJ.

"I'm sorry my sister got you over here," she said. "I'm fine."

"She was trapped in the woods in a blizzard with Silas Walker," Chloe said, as if TJ had to be reminded. "I asked the sheriff here because I want to know more about this man who had my sister, especially since he'd been fired from the police force."

McCall smiled and declined the coffee Annabelle offered her. The two were on a first name basis after what Annabelle had found in the house last month.

"I could use a cup," TJ said as they all sat down.

"Silas bought some land in the Little Rockies about six months ago," the sheriff said once they were settled in. "I believe he built a cabin." McCall looked to TJ, who nodded. "Yes, he was fired from the New York City police force as part of an internal sting operation." Chloe looked at TJ as if to say "See?"

"But Silas was innocent. He was working undercover on behalf of the department to root out the dirty cops."

"That sounds dangerous," Chloe said.

All TJ could think about was the man who'd

served her homemade bread and stew he'd made himself. The man who wrote beautiful words, deep with meaning. A man with many talents.

McCall continued. "He was offered his job back, but he declined because a cop who testifies against his own isn't necessarily welcomed back with open arms. There was an attempt on his life. He was shot. He is now employed part-time by another former police officer who started his own private investigative business."

TJ realized that she hadn't been the only one limping. But Silas had been trying hard not to show it.

"Have you met him?" Chloe asked McCall, clearly still skeptical.

"I have," the sheriff said. "I found him to be quite delightful." She looked to TJ, who nodded before picking up her coffee cup. She could feel both of her sisters watching her intently.

"I hope that answers any concerns you have about the man. But your sister told me that you've been getting threatening letters from one of your fans," the sheriff said, meeting TJ's gaze.

She nodded. "I was worried Silas might be the fan."

"But you're not now?" McCall asked.

"No, I'm not." After hearing what the sheriff had to say, she realized she could trust her instincts about Silas. Her new instincts that told her he wasn't True Fan. Not that he wasn't dangerous to her. Just the thought of him made her heart beat a little faster.

"Well if you need anything, you know where my office is," McCall said as she got to her feet.

TJ said she did and was glad when Chloe walked the sheriff to the door.

"Well?" Annabelle said the moment their older sister was out of earshot. "What happened?"

"Nothing happened."

Annabelle rolled her eyes. "How did you end up at his cabin?"

Chloe had returned after seeing the sheriff out. "Yes, how did that happen?"

TJ recounted seeing the mailbox by the road and wandering back into the woods, curious about him. "I didn't realize how far I'd gone and the blizzard was getting worse. I fell and twisted my ankle. Fortunately, he helped me into this cabin. By then it was snowing too hard to drive out so he suggested I stay the night."

"Why do I suspect there is more to the story?" Annabelle asked.

"He was very nice, charming actually, and he fed me homemade stew and bread that he'd made and we played cards until it got late."

Her sisters exchanged a look. "Have you for-gotten that you thought he was True Fan?" Chloe demanded.

"No," TJ said. "And at first I thought he was. But none of that matters now. You heard the sheriff. There is nothing to worry about with him." They both looked at her as if they weren't convinced. "Isn't it possible that he's just a nice man who still wants to help me?"

"What does that mean?" Chloe asked.

"He's determined to help me find True Fan," she said with a shrug.

"Seriously?" Annabelle asked, eyes widen-ing. "He is awfully good-looking if you like that big, muscled, chisel-jaw kind of man."

"I would be very careful," Chloe said. "Even if he isn't True Fan, this man could still be dangerous."

"You mean dangerous to someone as naive as me?" TJ said, bristling because she'd figured that out all on her own—but wasn't about to admit it.

Her sister seemed to take her time answering as if taking care with her words. "You haven't dated since Marc. That's all I'm saying."

She wanted to argue that Chloe had no idea how many men she'd dated, since they didn't live in the same city. But she saved her breath. Her sister was right. She hadn't dated since Marc. He'd been her college boyfriend. Her first. Her last. Their senior year at university, he'd gotten a job with a defense contractor working in high-risk countries.

The plan had been that she would kick-start her writing career and they would get married after he had an adventure and made a lot of money. She hadn't liked the plan, but Marc had been so excited, saying he needed to live a little dangerously before he could settle down. He'd been killed in Iraq when the company office where he worked was bombed.

"I'm only saying that I don't think you want another man who lives that close to the edge," Chloe said quietly.

TJ felt tears burn her eyes. Her sister was right. Silas Walker had gone into a dangerous profession and even volunteered to go undercover to weed out dirty cops. Just as Marc had felt the need for adventure in danger zones in the world.

"Don't worry," she said, more to herself than to her sisters. "I won't make the same mistake again."

A knock at the door relieved the tension in the kitchen. "I'll get it," Annabelle said, jumping to her feet.

TJ stayed where she was. She couldn't help thinking about how gentle and caring Silas had been. And yet from the first she'd sensed that darkness, that violence, that menace. Was she doomed to be attracted to men who liked to risk their lives?

Annabelle returned on a gust of cold air. TJ had her back to the door but she saw from Chloe's expression that something was wrong.

"Who was that at the door?" Chloe asked.

"It was Carol again from the post office," Annabelle said.

TJ didn't need to turn around. She knew without seeing the letter in her sister's hand. True Fan had sent her another threat.

SILAS DROVE AROUND Whitehorse street by street, looking for the house where he'd picked up the reams of paper at the garage sale. Whitehorse was only ten blocks square so it didn't take long to find the house where he remembered stopping at the garage sale.

He pulled up out front, got out and started toward the front door. As he did, he saw a front curtain twitch. A moment later, he knocked at the door and waited. He knocked again.

A small elderly woman opened the door a crack. "Yes?" she asked.

"Hello." He smiled, but she still looked wary. He couldn't remember the woman who had sold him the reams of papers, but he was pretty sure it wasn't this one. The house had been for sale because the owner was moving into the rest home as he recalled.

"Who is it, Mother?" said a younger voice from behind the woman.

"I don't know."

The door opened wider as another hand appeared on the edge of it.

"Can I help you?" asked a woman a good thirty years younger.

"I was looking for the woman who used to live in this house," Silas said. "She had a garage sale here last summer?"

The younger of the two nodded. "Melinda Holmes. She moved into the rest home." She pointed down the street.

"Thank you." He started to turn away.

"You bought something at her garage sale?" the woman asked, clearly curious why he would be looking for Melinda Holmes about dealing with an item from last summer's garage sale.

"Reams of paper," he said, turning back.

"Oh." She looked disappointed. Had she been hoping for a chest with a secret in it? Or something of more value that he might have wanted to return? Whatever she'd been hoping for, those hopes dashed, she closed the door.

Glancing at his cell phone, he saw that it was still early. He drove over to the house where he'd dropped off TJ earlier. Getting out, he walked to the door, wondering what kind of reception he would get not only from her, but also from her sisters.

He climbed the stairs to the porch and knocked. The young woman who opened the door was blonde and blue-eyed. There was just enough resemblance that he knew she was one of TJ's sisters.

"Hi," he said, and smiled. "I was hoping to see—" Just then another sister appeared, followed by the one he'd come for. His smile broadened as TJ came into view.

"Silas," she said, sounding a little breathless as if she'd just raced down from upstairs. There was an awkward moment where they all stood there looking at him. The sisters were definitely giving him the once-over.

"Please, come in," TJ said, shooing her sisters aside. He wiped his feet and, removing his Stetson, stepped into the house. "I don't think you've met my sisters. This is Chloe, who's an investigative reporter, and Annabelle, who is—"

"Just Annabelle now," the young woman said.

"I was going to say, just nosy," TJ finished.

All three were beautiful alone, but together they made quite a sight.

"This is Silas Walker," TJ said almost shyly.

He nodded to the other two women. "Nice to meet you."

"Can we offer you some coffee?" Annabelle asked.

"Thanks, but I'm fine. I just came by to tell your sister…" his gaze went to TJ "…that I found that house we talked about. The owner is in the local rest home. Melinda Holmes. Do you know her?"

"She should, since you used to steal the apples out of her tree on the way home from school," Annabelle said with a laugh. "I wonder if she'll remember you."

"Isn't that the woman who beat you with the broom as you were climbing her fence?" Chloe asked.

"Ah, the memories," TJ said as she reached

for her coat. "I'd love to stay and reminisce but I have to find True Fan."

"If you haven't already found him," Chloe said under her breath.

Silas merely smiled, said how nice it was to meet them and TJ closed the door behind them. He saw that she'd showered and changed into jeans, boots and a sweater under her coat. Her blond hair was brushed and now floated like a golden cloud around her shoulders.

"I apologize for my sisters," she said. "They're...protective."

He chuckled. "You should be thankful for that." Glancing over at her, he grinned. "You really did steal apples from this woman we're going to see?"

"Let's hope the reason she's in the rest home is because she has forgotten the past," TJ joked.

"Not too far into the past though," he said as he opened the passenger side of his pickup. "We need to know who all she sold paper to."

THE REST HOME sat on a hill overlooking White-horse and the Milk River drainage. The valley was covered in trees that seems to follow the river northward. Silas parked and started to get out, when she stopped him.

"I got another letter."

"Let's see it." He heard the fear in her voice, but when he turned to look at her, she looked deceptively calm. However, as she opened her purse and removed the envelope, he saw that her fingers were trembling.

Silas carefully opened the envelope and pulled out the letter, trying not to touch it more than necessary. He wondered if TJ had taken the same precautions or if all three of the sisters had manhandled it. Not that he thought there would be fingerprints on it. With all the crime shows on television now, only a fool would send an anonymous threatening letter and leave behind evidence of the sender.

Tessa Jane,

I had such expectations for you and your books. I am sick over what has become of you—let alone what you have dragged your characters through. I knew you would corrupt Constance. For a while, she was the best of you.

Not anymore. That she could kill Durango... That YOU could kill him. He was the good in Constance. How could you not see that? You took a beautiful thing and ruined it.

I told you I was your only True Fan until the end. Well, I'm afraid this has to end. I can't let you write another book. I'm sorry, but you've abused your talent, and for what? Fame? Fortune?

You've been playing God with your characters—and your readers.

It's time to pay the piper.

SILAS FELT FURY roiling up deep inside him. Who was this crazy person? And more important, just how dangerous was True Fan?

He looked over at TJ. She'd gone pale, as if remembering each word of the letter as he was reading it. He told himself it didn't matter how crazy this person was or if they were serious about their threats of violence; they had to be stopped. He could tell that TJ was terrified. He couldn't imagine what it must be like for her to try to write another book with this hanging over her.

"All right if I keep this for now?" he asked as he carefully put the letter back into the envelope. She nodded as if she wanted nothing to do with it. "When is your next book due?"

"Four months from now. And no, I have nothing done on it," she said. "I might have to buy back the contract—if my publisher will let me."

He swore under his breath. "Let's hope Melinda Holmes has some answers for us," he said as he opened his door.

TJ HAD FELT sick to her stomach since opening the letter from True Fan. But having Silas helping her made her feel stronger as they entered the rest home. She'd been surprised that he'd moved so quickly on this. She hadn't expected him to go in search of the garage sale house so fast.

But she was thankful that he had and that he was taking the threats seriously. Once inside the rest home they were directed to Melinda Holmes's room. Unfortunately it was empty. A passing nurse told them to try the dining room.

They found her sitting by the window staring out at the winter day. TJ barely remembered her from the broom-swinging woman who'd pounded her backside as she scrambled over the wooden fence behind the Holmeses' house.

"Mrs. Holmes?" Silas asked. No reaction. "Mrs. Holmes?" he said a little louder.

The elderly gray-haired woman turned from the window. "I'm not deaf," she snapped, her narrowed gaze going from Silas to TJ. "I know you," she said in a hoarse voice as her gaze bored into TJ. "You're one of those wild Clementine girls. You've been in my apples again, haven't you?"

"You grow the best apples in the valley," she said as she took a seat next to her. "This is my friend Silas."

Melinda's gaze shifted to him. "You stealing my apples too?"

"No, ma'am. I wouldn't do that."

His answer seemed to satisfy her. "So what do you want, then?"

"You're the woman who used to own the

store here in town that sold paper supplies, right?" Silas said.

"That was years ago."

"I bought some reams of paper from you at your garage sale last summer."

She looked from him to TJ as if to say, "So?"

"Do you remember who all you sold the paper to?" he finished.

She looked suspicious. "Why? There wasn't a thing wrong with that paper. Might have been a little discolored, that's all. Some of it got wet, but it dried out just fine."

"It was great paper. In fact," Silas continued, "I'd like to see if I can find more of it. I thought some of the people who bought it might make me a deal."

Melinda Holmes seemed to appreciate a man who liked a good deal. "A lot of people were at that garage sale. You expect me to remember after all this time?" She huffed at that. "There was that one woman from the school.

She bought a few reams. Probably all gone now since she said she was going to give it to the school district to use."

"You don't remember her name?" TJ asked.

"Never knew it," she snapped without looking at her. Her face was set in a grim line and for a moment TJ thought that was all they were going to get.

"Then there was Nellie," the elderly woman said as if there hadn't been a break in the conversation. "She bought my bowl set. It had belonged to my mother." The woman bit her lower lip for a moment looking as if she might cry, before she said, "And there was that maddening Dot." She shook her head. "That woman has always annoyed me since she was a child. And that one fella… Sulky and kind of creepy as a boy—you know who I'm talking about," she said, turning to TJ. "He used to follow you girls home every day from school. He seemed to favor you."

"Tommy Harwood." TJ had known who she was referring to right away even though she hadn't realized that he'd followed them every day from school. She'd only caught him at it a few times.

"That's all I can remember," Melinda said, clearly finished with them. She turned back to the window.

TJ and Silas rose and left. "For someone with a bad memory she did well, I'd say," he said with a laugh. "You know these people she was talking about?" She nodded as they climbed into the pickup. "Could one of them be True Fan? Maybe this creepy kid who used to follow you home?"

"Maybe. I think I heard he lives by the railroad tracks on the way out of town," she said. "But he wouldn't be home now. He works at the auto shop. But Nellie should be home. Do you want to try her?"

Lanell "Nellie" Doll answered the door, opening it only a few inches. Still TJ saw enough of the inside to see that the woman's mother, who she lived with, was much like TJ's own grandmother—a hoarder.

"What are you doing here?" Nellie asked suspiciously.

"I stopped by to make sure you got the book I signed for you," TJ said.

"I did." She looked at Silas, clearly still waiting for an explanation.

"That wasn't the only reason we stopped by," Silas said. "Last summer I bought some paper at a garage sale from Mrs. Holmes. She thought you might have bought some as well and might have some extra still."

"Paper?"

"Mrs. Holmes sold it by the ream."

"If I bought some, I can't remember," Nellie said. "I probably used it up by now."

"I'm sorry, I should have introduced my friend," TJ said. "This is Silas Walker. He's a writer. Along with inexpensive paper, he was looking for a good manual typewriter."

"And Mrs. Holmes thought I might have that as well?" Nellie asked, sounding indignant. "That old woman should mind her own business."

"If you do have either, I would be happy to buy them," Silas put in.

Nellie was shaking her head. "I don't have any paper or a typewriter to sell. I'm busy so if that's all…"

"Have you started reading my book?" TJ asked before Nellie could close the door in her face. She was odd and secretive enough that she could definitely be True Fan. Not to mention unfriendly.

Nellie rolled her eyes with an impatient sigh. "If you must know, I don't care for your books. But my niece knows that we went to school together. Yesterday was my birthday so she thought it would make a nice gift to have you sign it for me."

"I see," TJ said, trying not to laugh. This was too funny. She loved the woman's honesty. "So you didn't read at least the first one I wrote, out of curiosity?"

"I couldn't get through it. But I never was much of a reader."

TJ could hear the drone of the television in the background and recognized the sound of a daytime drama. They were keeping Nellie from her "soaps."

"We're sorry to have bothered you," TJ said and Nellie quickly closed the door.

"Well, that was fun," Silas said as they climbed into the pickup.

TJ chuckled. "Wasn't it though."

"You went to school with her?"

"We weren't friends," she said unnecessarily.

He laughed. "I would have never guessed."

"I think we can scratch her off our list,' she said.

"I don't know about that. She definitely has some hostility issues."

TJ looked out the window at the town where she'd grown up. "Some of the people I went to school with thought I was stuck-up. Annabelle was stuck-up, but me?" She shook her head. "I was shy. Introverted. I've always had stories going in my head, which were more interesting to me than school. I remember being called on by the teacher and not having a clue what she'd been talking about. I'm sure the teacher and the other students thought I was slow if not stupid. My teachers used to tell my grandmother that I didn't apply myself."

"Me, I actually didn't apply myself." He shrugged and started the pickup. "Dot next?"

"Dorothy Crest? It seems unlikely that it would be her, but I guess that's the point. Whoever True Fan is, it's someone who is hiding behind anonymity."

"True Fan is probably capable of putting on a good front to your face. The fact that he or she doesn't sign his or her name makes me think that True Fan is a coward and probably not dangerous—at least face-to-face. But if they undermine your writing then they have to be dealt with."

She smiled over at him. "Then by all means let's go see Dot." She put in a call to Annabelle, who informed her that Dot had bought her parents' house and now lived in it with her husband, Roger. With Roger at work, TJ figured they would find her alone. She was right.

Dot came to the door in an apron, throwing it open, all smiles when she saw them. "Come in! This is such a treat. A real live famous author in my home."

TJ introduced Silas.

"You write as well? Wonderful. You'll have

to tell me the title of your latest book so I can pick it up. I love to read when I have time, which isn't often keeping up this house, you know."

She led them through the living room, pointing out that she had all of TJ's books on a special shelf of their own. The house was immaculate even though Dot kept apologizing for the mess.

In the roomy farm-style kitchen, she offered them cookies straight from the oven and coffee, saying that the coffee was always on at her house.

TJ took a warm chocolate chip cookie and listened while Silas visited with Dot. He asked about the paper she'd bought at the garage sale last summer, adding, "I think that's where I saw you before." He told her he'd been using his to write a novel on.

"I gave mine to the grandchildren. They love to draw and go through so much paper."

TJ was glancing around the kitchen when Dot said, "You've never seen my house. Would you like a tour?"

"I'd love one," she said, and got to her feet. The rest of the house was just as spotless as what TJ had already seen. In what appeared to be a den, she saw a laptop, but no typewriter.

"I'm halfway through your new book. I had to quit because I wasn't going to get my work done." Dot shook her head. "But I didn't want to put it down. I'm in awe of the way you make our little town come alive."

"You do know that the books aren't about Whitehorse," TJ said.

"Of course." She gave TJ a wink.

"They're supposed to be any small town in Montana."

Dot either ignored her or didn't hear her. "I'm so glad you stopped by with your friend. I'd seen him around but I had no idea he was a writer."

TJ found it amusing that when locals called him a mountain man they were a little leery of him. But now that they would soon know he was a writer, his mountain man appearance would be accepted as just the way writers were.

They found Silas sitting where they'd left him in the kitchen, but TJ had the feeling that he'd looked around the lower floor while they'd been gone.

They thanked Dot and left, but only at her insistence that Silas take a few cookies for later.

"It's her," he joked as they drove away. "All that cheerfulness has got to be hiding something."

TJ chuckled. "I had the same thought," she said as she settled back against the seat. The sun shone in the pickup's side window. She felt warm and content and realized she hadn't felt like this in months—except in this man's presence.

"Any other leads we should follow up, or should we have lunch?" he asked.

"You probably have other things you need to do," TJ said.

"The sooner we find this creep, the better," he said.

But as he drove down the main drag of Whitehorse, she saw him suddenly look in the direction of a man crossing the street ahead of them—and freeze for a moment.

"Silas?"

He didn't answer.

"Is everything all right?" she asked, fearing what now had him looking like a man who'd seen a ghost.

He seemed to come out of his fugue state as the vehicle in front of them that had been waiting to turn finally moved. The man who'd crossed the street was now nowhere to be seen.

He appeared to have stepped into the Mint Bar. "Sorry, I just thought I saw... Never mind. It wasn't who I thought it was."

But she caught him looking back at the bar and later watching his rearview mirror as if he thought they might have been followed. Whoever he'd thought the man was, his reaction had been powerful. Silas was still spooked and she had a feeling he didn't scare easily.

Chapter Thirteen

Silas glanced at his phone and groaned inwardly. He was still shaken. The last thing he wanted to do was cancel out on TJ. But right now he had to take care of some business—and quickly.

"I'm sorry. There's something I need to see about right away," he said to her. "Can I take a rain check on lunch? I'll call you later."

"You don't need to go see this Tom Harwood with me. I appreciate you finding the house where you got the paper. I can take it from here."

That's what worried him. "I don't like you

doing this on your own. I'll take care of my business, then check with you later, if that's okay."

"Of course. But are you sure everything is all right?" she asked, looking worried. She'd seen his reaction to the man crossing the street. He felt bad enough that the man might have seen him—and TJ. He didn't want her dragged into his dirty business.

"I'm fine. We'll talk later," he said, smiling over at her. He must not have been as convincing as he'd hoped, because she still looked worried.

"I need to go Christmas shopping with my sisters, so please, take care of whatever you need to, and don't worry about me."

He glanced over at her, his heart breaking a little with worry over her. "I can't help but be concerned. That last letter…" What he wanted to say was, "We have to find True Fan before True Fan finds you," but he held his tongue. She was already scared enough. She didn't need him sharing his instincts or experience with her.

Unfortunately, those instincts and his experience on the job told him that True Fan would be making good on those threats—and soon.

As he pulled up in front of her house, he turned to her and reached for her hand. "Do me a favor, okay?" She nodded, seeming surprised by how serious he'd become. "Don't go anywhere alone. Take one of your sisters if you insist on going out. Especially don't go chasing True Fan. Wait for me. I'm not sure how long my business is going to take me but—"

"You don't have to worry about me. I'll be fine."

How many times had he heard those words? "That's what they all say." He felt her shudder. "Just do it for me."

TJ FELT HER throat constrict. Silas was so worried about her that it gave her a chill. "I will.

But promise me something," she heard herself say. "Be careful. I don't know what this business is you have to take care of, but I'm betting it's dangerous from your reaction back there."

He said nothing for a moment, just squeezed her hand. "I'll call you later."

She nodded as he let go of her hand. For a moment she was afraid to leave him. But he reached over and opened her door and all she could do was look at him for a moment before climbing out. It felt so strange to feel this close to someone she'd met only hours before. She was making her way toward the house when she heard him drive away. There was an urgency about his leaving that made it all the more frightening.

What kind of trouble was Silas in? Something to do with his former job? Or something to do with his more recent one as a private investigator? She knew so little about him and yet she felt she knew him. Just the first chapter of his novel had made her feel closer to him. She could understand why readers thought they knew her and feared some of them did.

Her heart ached as she turned to watch his pickup disappear around a corner.

"Well?" Chloe said from the open doorway.

"Is that what you're going to say to me every time I return to the house?" TJ demanded as she stepped past her and into the warmth of the living room.

"It is if every time you leave it's with that man," her sister said.

Annabelle called from the kitchen that she'd made sloppy joes for lunch and TJ was just in time. Taking off her coat and dropping it on a chair in the living room, she followed the sweet, temping scent into the kitchen.

"I haven't had sloppy joes since I left White-horse," TJ said as she helped set the table. Chloe was standing in the doorway, arms crossed, looking upset. That was the problem

with mystery writers and investigative reporters, TJ thought. *We see things other people
miss.* Chloe knew there was more to Silas.
She'd seen the darkness, the danger.

"Silas found the house where he bought
reams of paper last summer at a garage sale,"
she said as she took a seat at the table. Annabelle brought over the dish of sloppy joes and
put it on the table before taking a seat. Chloe
joined them, though with some reluctance.

"The paper is the same paper True Fan uses
to write me letters," TJ said. "Or at least it
looks to be the same. So we asked who'd
bought some of it at the garage sale last summer."

"And?" Chloe said. She hadn't touched her
lunch yet.

"She gave us a few names. Dot, Nellie Doll,
someone from the school and Tommy Harwood were the ones she could remember. She
said Tommy used to follow us home from

school all the time." She turned to Chloe. "Do you remember that?"

Her sister nodded. "He had a crush on you." She frowned. "Wasn't he at the signing?"

"He was." TJ took a bite of her lunch. "Annabelle, this is delicious. I didn't realize how hungry I was."

"So did you talk to the others?" Chloe asked.

"We didn't get a chance to talk to more than Nellie and Dot," she said, not looking up from her meal. "Silas had some business he had to take care of. He's going to call later." She lifted her gaze to meet Chloe's dark blue one. "He isn't True Fan."

"No, but he certainly has taken an interest in finding this person, hasn't he?"

TJ shrugged. "Maybe he's more interested in me."

Annabelle's eyes went wide. "So something *did* happen at the cabin. Did he...kiss you?"

TJ laughed. "No, and nothing else happened

either. He was a perfect gentleman." She saw that Chloe felt that proved her point that Silas was in this just for the excitement. For the possible danger. That he was like Marc.

"So are we going Christmas shopping this afternoon?" she asked, hoping to change the subject.

"I thought we'd walk since it is such a nice day," Annabelle said. "I want to find something for Dawson. I need your opinion. I found a shirt down at Family Matters. But is a shirt too unexciting for our first Christmas together—well, first this time around?" she added with a giggle.

It was impossible not to smile at their sister's happiness. Even Chloe, whose brow had been knitted with worry, broke into a smile.

"I'll have to see this shirt," Chloe said, and finally began to eat her lunch.

TJ tried to relax. She hadn't told them about Silas's reaction earlier or her fears. She'd gotten close to this man so quickly. That alone should have been a red flag. That Silas was in some sort of trouble seemed more than likely. He'd tried to play it down, but she'd seen how scared he'd been. What did it take to scare a man like him?

She tried to put him out of her mind. It hadn't been that hard with other men she'd met and even dated. But Silas… There was something special about him. And yet, Chloe's fear that he was too much like Marc kept nagging at her. She couldn't go through that again. Her heart couldn't take it.

"You're sure it was him?"

Silas held the phone more tightly in his hand. "Not positive. I only got a glimpse of him."

"Okay," said his friend and employer at the PI agency Cal Barnum. "First things first, I'll see if he's still out here in New York. This town you're in, it's small, right?"

"It doesn't even have a stoplight."

"So there is little chance he just happens to be there?"

"None. If he's here, then he's come for me."

"Maybe you should make yourself scarce," Cal suggested.

Any other time, Silas would have taken that advice. "It isn't that simple right now. I'm helping a friend with a problem she has."

"A friend? A new *female* friend, I take it?"

"She's in trouble. I can't just drop it."

"Okay, so how long before DeAngelo finds you?"

Silas pulled off his Stetson and raked a hand through his hair. He'd figured out how small towns worked pretty quickly after moving here. People weren't suspicious. They were annoyingly helpful. Looking for someone? Hell, they'd draw DeAngelo a map to his cabin.

"I'm going to have to find *him*," he said.

Cal swore. "I'm sorry. You knew it was just

a matter of time. From the start, you'd been suspicious of that crazy bastard Nathan De-Angelo."

Silas and Nathan had been thrown together as partners when Silas had started with the force. Nathan had been there for a while and had promised to teach him the ropes. It hadn't taken any time at all to see that his partner liked cutting corners.

"I'd hoped he'd have the sense to let it go," Cal was saying.

"That isn't his way." He put his hat back on, his mind already working. He had little choice. He'd have to run DeAngelo to ground—or wait at the cabin for the man to come gunning for him. Silas had never been good at waiting.

"Let me know if you hear anything I should know," he said to Cal.

"Keep in touch and…good luck."

It was going to take more than luck. He knew DeAngelo well. He'd helped bring the man down for his crimes. But when it came to hard time, the man had slipped the noose. Too many friends in high places. Too much dirt out there that DeAngelo was holding over even those in the judicial system.

So where to begin looking for the man? Although that wasn't the main question on his mind. *What are you going to do when you find him?*

TJ TRIED NOT to worry about Silas as she and her sisters walked uptown. Annabelle was right. It was a beautiful December day, the sun shining, the new snow so pure white and sparkling. Christmas decorations adorned all the houses they passed and each of the stores along the main drag of Whitehorse.

"We should drive down to Billings," Chloe said, not as enamored with the small Western town as her sisters.

"This is so much better than the rat race in

the largest city in Montana," Annabelle said, and laughed because all three of them lived in cities that made Billings seem small.

"Okay, come see this shirt I found for Dawson," she said, dragging them into the clothing store.

TJ spotted her former high school English teacher looking at scarves and quickly stepped behind the racks of clothing to escape. By now Ester would have finished the book. TJ didn't want to discuss the theme or her mistakes in grammar. Ester was one of those teachers who couldn't help wanting to continue to teach even in retirement.

Annabelle held up the shirt she'd picked out. "What do you think?"

It was a blue checked Western shirt. "It looks just like him," TJ said.

"I'd just buy him a rope. He's going to need it, married to you," Chloe joked. TJ was glad to see that her older sister had quit worrying about her for the moment.

"What does that mean?" Annabelle demanded. "That he'll want to hang himself or that he'll have to hog-tie me to keep me on the ranch?"

"I hadn't thought of either of those, but you have a point," Chloe said. "Buy the shirt. He won't care. He adores you and anything you give him, he'll love it."

Annabelle still looked skeptical. She shifted her gaze to TJ who smiled and nodded. "What he really wants for Christmas is you."

"I need to go down to the gift shop," Chloe said after Annabelle bought the shirt and had it wrapped and they exited the store. Annabelle said she wanted to look in the gift shop as well.

TJ had no desire to go into a place that sold her books for fear of running into someone who wanted to talk about the latest one. She knew killing off Durango was going to cause some readers to be upset. But she had to take the books where they led her.

Also, she had no desire to see Joyce Mason again. She considered her for a moment as True Fan and couldn't imagine the woman going to the trouble to write her the threatening letters. Joyce was more of an in-your-face kind of person.

"I'm going to duck into the coffee shop," TJ said. "Why don't you meet me there when you're through?" They agreed and parted. She breathed in the winter day, her thoughts instantly returning to Silas. Worrying about him, she didn't even notice a figure step out of the alley until she was grabbed.

A hoarse voice whispered, "Don't scream. It's just me, your biggest fan."

Chapter Fourteen

Silas drove down the main drag, parking next to the city park. Whitehorse had been one of those spots along the railroad that had grown into a town. Because of that the unmanned depot sat beyond the small park on the other side of the tracks.

His senses were on alert as he got out of his truck and checked the street. With all the shoppers, the small town was bustling. DeAngelo couldn't have picked a better time. The rest of the year a large, dark-haired burly man wearing city clothes would have stood out from the locals and been easier to spot.

DeAngelo always wore expensive slacks and polished black shoes. He was obsessed with shoes and many times couldn't stop himself from stopping in the middle of the sidewalk to wipe away a spot on the leather.

Silas had been expecting him to show up for over a year. He'd thought it would be outside his apartment in New York City. Or maybe even *inside* his apartment. He'd been rigging his doors all these months, so sure that it was only a matter of time before they came face-to-face.

When that happened, he'd always told himself that he would have only a matter of seconds to make his move. In truth, he would probably not have any time at all. DeAngelo knew him too well. Also there was nothing to say that hadn't already been said in court. From the witness stand, DeAngelo had mouthed "You're a dead man" the last time he'd seen him.

But after a year had passed with DeAngelo back on the streets, Silas had thought maybe the man had wised up. Maybe even a little time behind bars had taught him that he didn't want a repeat appearance.

Silas should have known better.

And now DeAngelo had not only shown up in Montana, but also at the worst possible time. Now Silas had met TJ and promised to help her. Lately, he'd even let himself think he might have a chance at settling down, having a home, a family. He desperately wanted this chance to get to know Tessa Jane. He'd actually been thinking that he might have a future.

Now those thoughts mocked him. As long as there were DeAngelos in the world, he would never find peace, let alone chance falling for someone and starting a family.

He waited for a car to pass, then ran across the street to the last place he'd seen his former partner. Pushing open the door to the Mint Bar, he stepped into the warm beer-scented darkness.

TJ SCREAMED AND kicked as she tried to free herself from the person who'd grabbed her. The toe of her boot came in contact with bone.

"Damn, you didn't have to kick me."

She spun around to come face-to-face with Tommy Harwood. The scream died in her throat as she saw him rubbing at his shin as if she'd nearly broken his leg.

"You can't just grab someone like that," she said, furious with him for scaring her the way he had.

"I just wanted to get your attention."

Well, he'd done that.

He quit rubbing his leg and looked embarrassed. "I thought... I thought you might want to have a cup of coffee with me."

She'd been headed for the coffee shop, she

reminded herself. Also, hadn't she wanted to quiz Tommy about the ream of paper he'd bought? "I'll buy," she said. "For kicking you."

Grudgingly he agreed.

"You're not working today?" she asked after they'd ordered two black coffees and taken them to a table by the window.

"Got off early."

She realized that this could be the longest coffee date she'd ever had if the conversation was anything like this. She decided to get right to it. "I meant to ask you about some paper you bought last summer at a garage sale."

He seemed surprised by the question, but answered anyway. "At Melinda Holmes's house."

"So you remember." When he said no more and looked away, she said, "Do you own an old manual typewriter?"

He looked up then, his dark eyes boring into her. "Is that really what you want to talk about?"

"I'm looking for one to buy," she said.

"And you thought I'd have one?" He shook his head. "Why wouldn't you go out with me in high school?"

Seriously? "High school? Is that what you want to talk about?"

"Yes. You knew I had a crush on you. You weren't even famous then. You weren't even *popular*. So why not go out with me?"

He wanted to be honest? Fine. "Since apparently you followed me home every day after school you would know that I didn't date much. Also it was creepy, you always looking at me the way you did, not to mention the only time you asked me out was in the middle of Biology class. You expected me to say yes in front of everyone?"

"That wasn't my best moment, I'll admit, but you still could have said something after that."

"I wasn't interested. But I wasn't interested in anyone else either."

"You went out with Darwin."

"That was his junior prom. I double-dated with my sister Chloe. She forced me to go." TJ remembered the scratchy dress, the uncomfortable high heels, the whole awkward night right up and through Darwin's sloppy kiss. The memory made her shudder. "It was a mistake. One I wasn't about to repeat."

"So you were shy and awkward. So was I. You didn't even give me a chance."

"Tommy—"

"Tom."

"That is all history. I can't undo any of it. If I could, I would never have gone out with Darwin, all right?"

"But you might have gone out with me?"

She picked up her coffee cup. "So you don't have an old manual typewriter?"

"What if I do?" he asked challengingly.

"Then I'd like to see it."

THE BAR WAS dim enough that he had to walk halfway in to see everyone inside. He told himself that he'd recognize DeAngelo without any trouble. He was wrong. The man who turned around on his bar stool had changed. His dark hair had receded. His face was gaunt and pale, and he'd clearly lost weight. He didn't look healthy, let alone strong and dangerous.

"Took you long enough," DeAngelo said. "I see you got rid of your date," he said, looking past him. "So have a seat. You can buy," he said, patting the empty bar stool next to him. "We need to talk."

The last thing Silas wanted to do was have a drink with his former NYPD partner. From the beginning they were too different. Silas went by the book. DeAngelo never met a rule he didn't want to break. But even so, Silas had never dreamed just how crooked the man had become before it was over.

"We have something to discuss?" he asked without moving.

His former partner chuckled. "You were always as stubborn as a brick. Sit down. If I was here to…" he lowered his voice even though there was no one sitting close by "…kill you, you'd already be dead and we both know it."

That, Silas thought with a grimace, was true. He knew firsthand how dangerous this man was. A part of him was thankful that DeAngelo wanted only to talk. Silas had become complacent. Up here away from the city, he'd become too comfortable. He'd let his guard down. Given that DeAngelo was here, Silas knew he should be dead. So why hadn't his former partner made his move?

Sliding onto the bar stool, he nodded to the bartender that he'd take the same thing his "friend" was having. A few minutes later, two beers were plunked down in front of them.

"I've never seen you drink beer," Silas commented. "You always went for the hard stuff."

"Maybe I've changed."

He wouldn't bet the farm on that, but he said nothing as he took a swig of his beer from the bottle. "What are you doing here, Nathan?"

TOMMY HAD WANTED her to ride in his car with him, but TJ had insisted on meeting him at his house. She let him think she had her own car. She also let him know that she had to tell her sisters where she was going since she was supposed to be shopping with them.

"Whatever," was all he said as he headed for his pickup parked across the street.

TJ waited until he drove away before she started to go down to the gift shop to tell her sisters where she was going. It was the smart thing to do. If Tommy was True Fan, she had no business being alone with him, period—let alone being with him alone and with no one

knowing where she'd gone. So she was glad
when the first sister she came across was Annabelle.

"I'm running over to Tommy Harwood's,"
she said, making it sound casual. "I'll be back
soon. Shall we meet up before supper, maybe
go have a steak or something?"

"Dawson's mom invited us out, remember?"
Annabelle said. "You remember Willie and
she wanted to see you."

"Okay. I won't be long. I have my cell." With
that she left Annabelle looking at jewelry,
knowing she could be there for a while.

The walk to Tommy's house was only four
blocks down the side road that followed the
tracks out of town toward Glasgow. Back when
the towns along this stretch of new rails were
being named, whoever was in charge got tired
of coming up with ideas and simply spun a
globe and randomly picked. It was why there

were towns with names like Malta, Zurich, Havre and Glasgow.

Tommy's car was parked in front of a small neat white house. She tapped at the front door and it opened almost as if he'd been watching out the window for her.

"You *walked*?" He sounded appalled that she'd done that after turning down a ride with him.

"I decided to leave the car for my sisters. Anyway, it's such a nice day, I wanted to walk."

He shook his head and turned back into the house. She followed. The place was as neat inside as it had been outside. She wondered if there'd been a woman in his life at some point. Hadn't Annabelle told her that he'd lived with his mother for years until her death?

"Can I get you something to drink or eat?" he asked as she closed the door behind her.

She turned and seeing how nervous he was,

instantly became more nervous herself. Coming here had probably been a mistake. Knowing Annabelle she might not even remember where her sister said she was going.

"I just came to see the typewriter," she said, trying not to be rude, but not wanting him to get the wrong impression. "It's a gift for my sister Chloe."

"Yes, the typewriter," he said glumly. "It's in here." He led the way through the house. She found herself looking for possible weapons she could use against the man if needed. Tommy wasn't large but he looked strong. Definitely stronger than she was.

He'd reached the kitchen. She saw stairs that went down into the basement but had already decided she wasn't going down there. He could bring the typewriter up if that's where he kept it. She was beginning to doubt he even owned one and was beginning to suspect this had been a ruse to get her into his house. But if that was the case, then at least he wasn't True Fan.

"There it is," he said, not going near the basement stairs.

She looked to where he was pointing and saw an old manual Royal sitting on the floor in front of a door to the screened-in back porch.

"I use it for a doorstop. It weighs a ton," he said.

She stepped over to gaze down at the machine. It had an old, worn-out ribbon in it, but from the dust on the key arms it appeared it hadn't been used in years. "This is the only one you have?"

He gave her a disbelieving look. "You didn't come here to buy a typewriter. I know. I read your book."

That stopped her cold. She held her breath, always wary when this was the way someone began a conversation with her. *I read your book.* Sometimes that was all they said. But she had a feeling Tommy had a lot more to say.

Chapter Fifteen

"Look," Nathan DeAngelo said after taking a long gulp of his beer. Silas could tell it wasn't his first. "I don't blame you for what you did. I knew the kind of guy you were from the start. A Goody Two-shoes." He held up his hand before Silas could say what he was thinking. "Don't get me wrong. You did what you thought you had to do bringing us all down. But some of the guys aren't as…forgiving."

"This isn't news," Silas said, already bored with this conversation. He took a drink of his beer, wondering what had really brought his old partner all the way to Montana. Not to tell him something he already knew.

"I've moved on," DeAngelo continued. "I've got a pretty good gig going with a security company." He shrugged. "Keeps me out of trouble. The thing is, you taught us all an important lesson. We're not going to make the same mistakes again. We're not going to get our hands caught in the cookie jar again. That's why the guys all chipped in to hire a hit man to take you out. No way to trace it back to them."

Silas looked over at him and saw that he was serious. "And you came all this way to warn me."

"Like I said, I'm more forgiving." His gaze softened. "You and I were partners. The others can't believe you'd turn in your own partner. But I knew you would. I even suspected you were coming after us."

He shook his head. "I don't get it."

DeAngelo shrugged and drained his beer before pushing to his feet. "I can't explain it myself. Maybe I'm getting soft." He did look like he was. The security job obviously wasn't keeping him in as good of shape as the police department had. Or maybe he couldn't get his hands on the kind of drugs he'd had on the streets.

"Like you said, you could have killed me yourself and been on the next plane out of here. Why hire someone?"

"A professional seemed the way to go. Also we have something on the assassin so less chance of any blowback, you know what I mean?"

He did. "When?"

His former partner laughed. "Now what would be the fun of me telling you that?" He patted Silas on the shoulder. "Thanks for the beer. Almost like old times."

"One more thing," he said. "Did you chip in for the hit man as well?"

DeAngelo laughed and raked a hand through his thinning hair. "You know I did. Don't want them gunning for me next. It's bad enough that I didn't get the amount of time a lot of them did. And before you ask, no. No one knows I came up here to warn you. I know it's crazy, but I guess it's my way of saying I'm sorry. If you hadn't been so damned straitlaced we could have been great friends."

"I wasn't straitlaced. I just wasn't a dirty cop."

DeAngelo's smile blinked out, just like the light in his dark eyes. "See, you have to go and ruin a nice moment. Good luck." With that the man turned and walked away.

"I'M SORRY, BUT I don't have any idea what you're referring to," TJ said, just wanting to leave this house and Tommy. "You read my book and you know what?"

"Durango. I know why you killed him."

She hated to ask, but saw no way not to. "Why?"

"Because he wasn't the kind of man you wanted anymore."

"Tommy—"

"Tom."

"I'm not Constance. Durango died because he got cocky. He felt invincible. He forgot he was mortal." Also because Constance needed to move on from him. She needed another hero, maybe one not as flawed as Durango. Or maybe more flawed. She wouldn't know until she wrote the book.

"He was Marc, the guy you were engaged to in college," Tommy said.

She felt her face burn with irritation and embarrassment. That was one of the problems with a small town. People knew way too much of your business even after you left. Anger overtook her embarrassment. She didn't have to explain her actions to anyone, especially Tommy.

"I really don't want to talk to you about this," she said, and looked at her watch. Her sisters should be through shopping by now, or at least interested in eating.

"It's fine if you don't want to admit it," he said. "But if you ever quit making the same mistakes with men…"

She stared at him. True Fan told her how to write. Tommy was telling her how to run her love life? "Who are you to tell me who I should be with?" she demanded angrily.

"Just the man who's watched you make the same mistakes since you were a girl," he said, apparently unperturbed by her angry outburst.

"I can see myself out," she said, and spun on her heel, stomping out of the house. The walk back into town did her good, even though the temperature had dropped. The air smelled as if snow was imminent. She'd heard that yet another storm was coming in. Winter in Montana, she thought, and pulled her coat tighter around her.

She was almost back when a horn honked right behind her. She jumped, having not heard a vehicle approach. Turning, she told herself that if it was Tommy she would kick in one of his door panels.

But as the car pulled alongside, she saw it was her former English teacher Ester Brown. Great, she thought, as Ester whirred down her passenger side window.

"Why don't you get in," she said in a tone that made it clear it wasn't a question but an order. "It's too dangerous to walk along this road."

TJ bristled. A few too many people had been telling her what to do. She wasn't one of this woman's students anymore.

"Thanks, but no thanks. I want to walk so I'll take my chances getting run down on the road." She turned and stalked off, keeping to the edge of the road facing traffic so the elderly woman didn't mow her down on principle.

She heard Ester mumble, "Always was too stubborn for her own good," before she hit the gas and took off with the chirp of the tires.

Fortunately, town was only a short walk. She found her sisters coming out of the drugstore, both carrying an assortment of packages. They really had been Christmas shopping. She realized that she should be doing some of her own. But she couldn't get into a holiday mood—not with True Fan so close by.

"Where have you been?" Chloe asked with her usual suspicion.

"Didn't Annabelle tell you?"

Annabelle, who had been looking into one

of her bags she was carrying, looked up at the sound of her name.

"You didn't tell Chloe where I'd gone?" TJ chastised. What if Tommy had been True Fan? What if she was bound and gagged in his basement?

"Oops, sorry." Annabelle turned to Chloe. "She went to Tommy Harwood's house."

"Not all that helpful now, sis," TJ said.

"Why in the world would you do that?" Chloe cried.

"I thought he might be True Fan," she said, suddenly tired. She watched Ester Brown drive by, glaring at her as she passed and turned away from the street. She was reminded of all the reasons she'd left here, threatening never to come back. "Tommy gave me a lecture on my mistakes when it comes to the men I choose."

Both of her sisters lifted brows at that.

"I'm starved," Annabelle said quickly to change the subject before they got into an argument on the street. "Let's go to the Great Northern and have some lunch."

TJ looked up the street and saw Silas coming out of the Mint Bar. He spotted her and stopped. He'd been headed toward his pickup parked across the street when he saw her. Now he stood as if unsure what to do.

"You guys go on ahead. I'm tired and not hungry right now. I think I'm going to walk home." She headed toward Silas, ignoring Chloe's comment that for the first time Tommy Harwood might actually know what he was talking about.

Just the sight of TJ stopped Silas in his tracks. His spirits instantly lifted and just as quickly dropped. Nathan DeAngelo was a lot of things, a liar among them. But this time, Silas believed the man. He'd found over the years that there really was often some misguided honor among thieves. He also knew how much Nathan had hoped that Silas would adopt his way of thinking when it came to following the letter of the law.

"Hi," TJ said as she approached. She was frowning.

He realized that she'd seen him come out of the bar. She'd also seen his reaction earlier when he'd spotted DeAngelo crossing the street to the bar. She was too sharp not to have put it together.

As he looked into her beautiful face, he knew he had to keep his distance from her. It was bad enough that Nathan had seen him with TJ. He couldn't have his enemies using her against him. And at the same time, he couldn't just dump her unceremoniously.

The thought surprised him since it wasn't like they were a couple. But he'd promised to help her find True Fan and the one thing he'd lived by all his life was making good on his promises. He also couldn't put her in any more danger than he had and yet, seeing her, all he wanted to do was take her somewhere, just the two of them. He felt torn. While he shouldn't be with her right now, he also couldn't explain himself on the busy street.

A snowflake drifted down, followed by another large lacy one. His breath came out frosty white as he stepped to her. "Is there somewhere we can go and talk?" he asked. "Alone?"

She nodded and let him take her arm as they crossed the street to his pickup. Once inside, he started the engine, waiting for the heater to warm up enough to chase off the frosty chill in the cab. TJ hadn't said anything since climbing into the passenger seat. Outside, snow began to fall in a blur of white.

"I could take you to one of my favorite places outside of town," she said, breaking the quiet.

He looked over at her, telling himself all the reasons this was a bad idea and yet unable to simply walk away from her. The heater began to warm, clearing off the frost on the windshield enough that he would be able to see to drive.

Shifting the pickup into gear, he pulled out and followed her directions as they left town and headed northeast. Neither of them spoke as he drove. Snow blew across the highway. He recalled someone telling him they were called snow-snakes. It had a hypnotizing effect. He had to concentrate to keep the pickup on the highway as both the snow on the ground and the now falling snowflakes whipped around the truck.

They'd gone out of town some miles before she told him to turn. He checked his rearview mirror, not for the first time. He didn't believe they'd been followed. That was the problem with a small town. There was no reason to follow them. All the killer had to do was wait. It would be easy to find Silas's cabin. This was the kind of job even an amateur should be able to handle.

The road TJ had him turn onto went from snow-packed pavement to deeper snow-covered gravel before she told him to turn once more. He could see an expanse of flat white through the falling snow. As they neared it, he realized it was a frozen-over lake. He saw picnic tables covered with snow under the trees along the edge of the lake and pulled down into one of the campsites.

This one was somewhat sheltered by the trees. He left the engine running, knowing how quickly the cab would get cold without the heater, and watched the snow whirling around them. He liked the intimate feeling. He could almost pretend that they were the only two people on earth in the warm cocoon of the pickup's cab.

"You're in some kind of trouble, aren't you?" TJ said after a few moments.

He glanced over at her and simply nodded. "I can't let you get dragged into it so I'm going to have to stay away from you for a while."

"What if that isn't what I want?" she asked, her voice breaking.

He met her gaze. His blue eyes shone. "It is the last thing I want. I know I promised to help you find True Fan—"

"Is that the only reason?"

"I think you know better than that." He let out a frustrated sigh and reached over to brush a lock of her hair back from her face.

TJ CLOSED HER eyes at the warm caress of his fingertips on her cheek.

"Tessa Jane." He said her name like a curse, his voice thick with emotion. "All I can think about is you. You've completely captivated me."

She opened her eyes and met his blue gaze. Without another word, he reached for her, drawing her across the bench seat of the pickup. She felt a burst of pleasure expand inside her as he wrapped her in his strong arms and kissed her. His mouth was warm and sweet on hers.

"I've been wanting to do that since the first time I saw you," he said pulling back to look into her face.

She kissed him in response, weaving her fingers through the curls at his nape, breathing in the male scent of him. Desire sparked into a blaze inside her. She didn't care what Tommy or her sisters said. Silas was all man and more enticing than any she'd ever met. She felt safe in his strong arms and desperately wanted to lose herself in him.

He kissed her again, this time slowly, expertly. He deepened the kiss as he slid out from under the steering wheel to pull her onto his lap. She pushed aside his coat and opened the buttons on his shirt until she could press her palms to his rock-solid chest. She felt him shudder, desire a blowtorch in all that blue. Heat pulsed through her to her center.

Silas unzipped her coat and found his way to her bare breast. She arched against him as he thumbed the already hard nipple to an aching point. His hand slipped into her jeans and panties. He found the spot and she knew this had been building for some time because she cried out as the release came almost immediately.

He drew her to him, holding her as she felt the waves of release ebb through her, leaving her feeling weak. She started to reach for him, but he stopped her and kissed her tenderly. "I hadn't meant for it to go this far. The first time I make love to you, I don't want it to be in the front seat of my pickup. I want to take this up sometime soon." He touched her cheek, his fingertips warm, his gaze filled with desire.

He groaned and pulled back his hand. "We should get going."

She fixed her clothing, zipping her coat. Even with the heater going, the windows had fogged over. This was so not like her. She barely knew this man. This was the kind of thing that Constance would do. For some reason that made her smile to herself.

Silas slid back over under the wheel and turned up the heat. "I'm not going to be able to see you for a while." He glanced over at her.

"You're not going to tell me what kind of trouble you're in."

He shook his head as he reached over and caressed her shoulder for a moment. "I can't tell you how much I hate this. But while I'm worried about you and True Fan, being around me right now is more dangerous."

"I'm getting it narrowed down. I talked to Tommy Harwood today." She shook her head at the memory. Wouldn't Tommy love to know about this? She felt her face heat and looked out at the lake for a moment. "It's not him. I've reached a dead end."

"I thought by following the paper trail we might find this creep. I'm sorry. The paper didn't lead us anywhere."

She agreed. "Too many people could have gotten some of that paper even if they hadn't bought it at the garage sale. But I think you're right. True Fan is a coward." She turned toward Silas. "So take care of your trouble and don't worry about me."

"That won't be easy," he said as he removed his hand from her shoulder and got the truck going. She heard the worry in his voice and knew that whatever trouble he was in, it was serious.

Chapter Sixteen

Silas dropped her off at her house after another kiss. TJ could tell that he hadn't wanted to let her go any more than she had wanted to leave him. Their feelings for each other had happened so quickly, it scared her. But it also excited her. For the first time in her life, she was being adventurous. It felt good.

She thought about his kisses. It felt wonderful.

"I don't know when I'll see you again," he said, his voice rough with emotion. "But know that you won't be far from my mind."

She'd wanted to ask him how dangerous

this trouble was, but in her heart she knew. She'd seen how scared he'd been when he'd recognized the man crossing the street earlier. Someone from his past? Someone he'd helped put in jail? Whoever it was, the man was dangerous.

Her heart ached. She and Silas had just found each other and now... Both of them had someone who was clearly threatening to hurt them and it had thrown them together. Earlier, at the lake, that feeling of impending doom had pushed them together faster than either of them had wanted.

But there was no denying the chemistry between them. They'd bonded at the cabin. She thought of their card games late at night with a blizzard howling outside the cabin and hugged that memory to her, afraid she might never see Silas alive again.

"This is about those cops you put in prison, isn't it?" she asked.

He looked at her. She could see him fighting not telling her the truth. "Was that man in town to kill you?"

"No. Warn me."

Her chest felt as if an elephant had settled on it. "Can you go to the sheriff?"

He shook his head. "I have to take care of it myself."

"Oh, Silas."

He touched her cheek again. "I need you to be careful."

"You too." They locked gazes for a long moment before he reached over and opened her door. There was nothing more either of them could say.

She watched him drive away before making her way up the porch steps and into the house. Her sisters were in the living room. They'd opened a bottle of wine. Both looked up expectantly at her as she came in and hung up her coat.

"Oh no, you didn't," Chloe said.

TJ turned, feeling her face heat even as she denied it. "We kissed and made out some..."

Her sister groaned.

"Oh let her have some fun," Annabelle said.

As TJ joined them and poured herself a glass of wine, she found herself near tears with worry. "I like him."

"We can see that," Chloe said.

"You should invite him to the Christmas dance at the old gym," Annabelle suggested. "Everyone in town will be there. Dawson and I are going." She grinned, hugging herself.

"The two of you are killing me," Chloe said.

"Isn't there someone you were interested in at the newspaper?" Annabelle asked.

Their sister shrugged. "I dated some, but no, I've never met The One."

"How do you know?" Annabelle said, turning in her chair as she warmed to the subject. "Look at Dawson and me. I left him even when he bought a ring and asked me to marry him. I thought he'd never forgive me. He said I broke his heart." Her voice cracked with emotion and tears flooded her blue eyes. "But we found our way back to each other. What about your old boyfriend, Justin Calhoun?"

Chloe shifted uncomfortably in her seat. "He wasn't my boyfriend exactly. Anyway, that ship sailed a long time ago. Didn't he marry… what was her name?"

"Nicole Kent," Annabelle said. "But he didn't marry her. They were engaged—at least according to Nici—but they broke up. She married someone else, got divorced. She lives here with a couple of her sisters and their kids."

"You've certainly gotten caught up on local gossip," TJ said, and took a sip of her wine. "Didn't Tommy live with his mother for a long time?"

Annabelle laughed. "As a matter of fact, he

did. She died a few years ago and he sold her house and bought that one out by the tracks."

TJ looked over at Chloe. She seemed to be lost in thought. Justin? The two of them had seemed perfect for each other but Chloe had been on her way to college so nothing had come of it. But TJ had always wondered if Nicole Kent hadn't been the reason the two hadn't seen each other after that. She remembered the girl and felt a shiver. That one had always been trouble.

They all jumped at a knock on the door. Exchanging looks, TJ got up this time to answer it.

"You really should get a post office box," Carol said as she handed her the letter that had come for her. "You're going to get me fired."

"Thanks for bringing it by, but if anymore come—"

"Don't worry. I'll see that you get them." Carol turned on the step and, the bells she was wearing jingling, took off toward her vehicle. Carol always wore bells at work this time of year.

TJ looked down at the letter in her hand and realized her hand was shaking.

"Here, let me open that," Chloe said, taking the letter from her as TJ stepped back inside. She tore it open and pulled out the sheet, discolored like all the others.

This time True Fan didn't even bother with her name.

I told myself not to take it personally. But you have ignored everything I've told you. You seem to think you're so much smarter than me. You don't need my help. You never have.

All my attempts to make your books better have been ignored. You find me to be nothing more than a pest you can't seem to get rid of. Well, that will soon be over. I've tried to let it go. But in good conscience I can't let you go on the way you are.

I don't think of myself as a violent person. But someone needs to stop you. This time you've gone too far. I guess I'm going to have to do it myself since you didn't take my advice. You could have done the world a favor by taking your own life, but why would you listen to me now? I'm going to have to take care of this myself. There is apparently no one else.

There was no True Fan to the end. The letter just ended.

Chloe threw it down in disgust. "This person is crazy. I think it's time to take it to the sheriff." She got to her feet. "Do you have the other letters that have come since we've been here?"

TJ nodded. There was a chilling violence to the letter, as if the person had reached some breaking point. She hugged herself as her big sister made the call.

Annabelle took the empty wine bottle and glasses into the kitchen. She'd finished washing the glasses when there was a knock at the door.

THERE'D BEEN FEW times in Silas Walker's life that he hadn't known what to do. He prided himself on making quick decisions, the kind that had saved his life more than once. But right now he felt adrift. He had no idea who had been sent to kill him—not that it would make much of a difference if he did.

He'd like to think that DeAngelo had exaggerated about just how professional this hit man was. He hoped for an amateur. Or at least someone who would give him a fighting chance by being just bumbling enough to give him a slight edge.

As he drove through the falling snow back

toward the cabin, he considered his options. He could return to New York City. Or he could take his chances at the cabin. He couldn't get TJ off his mind. Right now, the last thing he needed was his mind on anything but staying alive.

Earlier, he and TJ had come close to making love in his pickup. He'd wanted her more than he'd wanted to stay alive at that moment. To find someone like her now, now when his life was on the line, seemed too cruel a cosmic joke. It made him more determined to come out of this kickin'.

He stopped at the turnoff where he still had good cell phone coverage and called his friend and boss. "I just had a visit from my former NYPD partner. My buddies hired a hit man to take me out."

Cal swore. "How can I help?"

"I thought there might be something on the

street. I'd like to know who this guy is and if he's already in Montana."

"I'll put my ear to the ground and see what I can find out. Aren't most of these old buddies still locked up?" his friend asked.

"A couple of them skated, but most of them are still behind bars, why?"

"You're talking cold-blooded murder. They knew some lowlifes on the street, but not hit men. I'd say they met someone while in the pen and contracted him. Let me see who recently got released and call you back."

Rather than hope for service at the cabin, Silas drove on into Zortman to the bar. He braved the storm and climbed out to go inside even though the last thing he wanted was alcohol. The place was packed with the approaching holiday and the weather. He found a small empty table near the door and sat down where he could see anyone who entered. When the waitress came over he ordered a beer and a burger, realizing he hadn't eaten all day.

He'd finished the burger and half of the beer when Cal called back. A boot-stompin' song was playing on the jukebox so he tossed down some money for the waitress and took the call down the hallway toward the men's restroom.

"I'm good friends with the warden at the local penitentiary," Cal said without preamble. "He says the dirty cops are in a wing by themselves fearing for their lives so they didn't have much contact with inmates. However, there was one they were seen talking to in the yard a few times. He recently got out. He's called Little Huey, a mean son of a bee who's done a lot of time for everything *but* murder. Real name's Herbert Jones. Caucasian, five foot nine, doesn't weigh a hundred and fifty pounds soaking wet, but rotten to the core."

"Might explain why he's so mean. Probably had to be at that size on the streets," Silas said.

"If it's him he'll try to shoot me in the back, blindsiding me rather than come right at me."

"That would be my guess. You won't see him coming."

SHERIFF MCCALL CRAWFORD read the letters twice before folding them and putting them back in their envelopes. "You say there have been others?"

TJ nodded. "A dozen or so over the past six months."

"More threatening than these?" the sheriff asked.

"Some. At first True Fan was complimentary, but then that began to change. I didn't listen to the advice the reader was offering."

"Your fan suggested suicide?" McCall asked.

"Highly suggested it so I didn't write any more books that I would be embarrassed by," TJ said.

"And what makes you believe this individual

might be in this area other than the postmark on the letter?"

TJ told her about the reams of paper that Melinda Holmes had sold after it had been stored for years in her basement. She told her about Nellie, Dot and Tommy, the people who had bought the paper that Melinda remembered. "It's a rather distinct color that would be hard to match."

The sheriff agreed. "Man or woman?"

"Sometimes I think man. Other times, woman. I have no idea."

"You had a book signing the other day. Anyone come through who made you suspicious?"

TJ laughed. "Everyone makes me suspicious. But I suspect it is someone with a connection to New York City since True Fan sent me a photo taken from the sidewalk outside my apartment. The person wanted me to know how close they were." She thought about mentioning being pushed into traffic but tended to agree with Silas that it might have been accidental.

"There are people in town with connections to New York," McCall said thoughtfully. "Others who have visited. Would be interesting to find out who might have asked one of them to take a photograph of her favorite author's apartment. Or if they did it themselves. Is that information public knowledge?"

"No, but Silas suggested that someone could have followed me from one of my book signings. I've done signings only blocks from my apartment and walked home afterward. I wasn't paying attention. Anyone could have followed me without my knowledge, waited on the street and seen me close my curtain before turning on a light on the third floor."

The sheriff nodded. "I noticed in one of your social media photos there is a pretty good view of the interior of your apartment. The curtains were open and I could see not only their design—but the building across the street. Probably wouldn't take anyone with a knowledge of the area long to find you."

TJ shivered. While she was writing about stalkers and killers and how they found their victims, there was one stalking her—and she'd probably made it easy for True Fan. She could have even given her stalker ideas on how to find her in her books.

"Mind if I take these with me?" McCall asked as she got to her feet, still holding the letters.

"Please take them," TJ said, and watched the sheriff pocket the envelopes. "You agree that it's someone here in Whitehorse?"

"It would certainly appear that way. Let me see what I can find out. If you get any more or you think of anything else, please contact me at once," the sheriff said.

"I will." TJ walked her to the door and stood

on the porch hugging herself against the storm as the sheriff drove away.

As she started to turn back inside the house, she looked out at the neighborhood wondering if she was being watched at this moment by True Fan.

SILAS FINISHED HIS call and rather than walk back through the bar, decided to exit through the back. He circled around to his pickup. He'd already checked out the clientele enjoying themselves in the bar and hadn't seen anyone suspicious, let alone Little Huey. He had looked for the man who would be sitting alone. Even if Little Huey tried to blend in, he would stick out like a sore thumb in Montana.

He'd been aware of that very thing when he'd first moved here. It hadn't mattered how he'd dressed; it wasn't as if he could just put on a Stetson, jeans and boots and no one would know he wasn't from here.

That's why he knew his would-be killer would be sitting alone nursing a drink. That's if he'd already gotten this far.

Now as he walked out into the cold snow, Silas tried to think like a killer. If he was after a man like him in a state he didn't know, where would he start?

He'd fly in, rent an SUV or a pickup. A town like Whitehorse had a ten trucks to one car ratio. Then he would drive up the three hours from the airport to the western town.

Then what? If he asked a lot of questions, people would notice and say something about it. So he'd come armed with not just weapons. He'd know as much of his victim's backstory as he could get out of the men who'd hired him.

So he'd know about the cabin outside of Zortman. Silas thought of his mailbox down by the road. He couldn't have made it easier for someone to find him. Look how TJ had found him in a blizzard.

Climbing into his pickup, he started the engine and let it run. Snow had piled up on the windshield and now frozen down. His wipers were covered with ice. He let the defrost run while he thought it out.

His would-be killer would have to come prepared for the weather. That might be tougher. Unless he'd been in a Montana blizzard he would have no idea how hard it was to see— let alone get around—in the deep snow. He would have had to have purchased good boots, snow gear, a hat, goggles. Even that might not save him if he got turned around in the storm or stuck on the road.

Most people, with towns so far apart, carried food, water, blankets and matches. Silas had taken to carrying a sleeping bag behind the seat of his pickup. He never knew when he might need it. Which was also why he carried the shotgun on the rack behind his head—and the pistol under his seat.

But neither would protect him if Little Huey shot him in the back.

He saw that some of the snow had melted on the windshield, but the wipers would have to be cleaned off. He started to climb out when through the small defrosted spot on his windshield, he saw a man exit an SUV and head toward the front of the bar.

Silas felt his heart drop like a stone. His buddies hadn't sent Little Huey.

Chapter Seventeen

Kenny "Mad Dog" Harrington. Silas thought about ending this right here and now as he watched the man go into the bar. Kenny hadn't seen him with the windshield still mostly covered with snow and ice.

Silas stayed where he was for a moment and then hit his wipers. Enough snow and ice came off that he could see well enough to drive. Eventually the falling snow would cake on the wipers and he'd have a blurry mess on his windshield, but right now that was the least of his worries.

He drove out of town, watching his rearview

mirror. Had Mad Dog already been out to his cabin? He would know soon enough. On the way, he tried to think. Little Huey would have been waiting in the trees to ambush him. Mad Dog was a whole other breed of violent criminal. He'd come head-on. It would take a cannon to stop the crazy bastard.

Turning on to the road into his cabin, he saw that there were two sets of tracks. Someone had gone in—and come back out. Mad Dog had been to his cabin. Which meant he would be back. Silas had no idea how much time he had to get ready for the killer.

His mind raced as he drove, all the time keeping an eye on the rearview mirror. No Mad Dog yet. Maybe he would have a few drinks, snort some coke or take some uppers. Silas knew how hard it was to stop a junkie. A junkie with Mad Dog's size and determination would be almost impossible to stop even filled with lead shot. But Silas had no choice unless…

He was almost to the cabin when a plan began to crystallize. It would be damned risky. Crazy under other circumstances. But worth a shot, he told himself as he pulled in front of the cabin and cut the engine. He would have to move fast. He had one thing going for him: Mad Dog wasn't smart. Also it was snowing so hard, his tracks would be covered quickly.

TJ's CONCERN FOR Silas had been growing by the hour. The thought of him alone at the cabin was driving her crazy. She kept telling herself that he was an ex-cop; he could handle himself. But she'd seen his reaction to the man.

"Can you sit still for five minutes?" her sister Chloe snapped. "This is about Silas Walker, isn't it? What has you so worked up?"

She wasn't about to tell Chloe. Her sister already thought that he was the wrong man for her. If she knew the danger he was in right now… "We left things a little…up in the air," she said truthfully.

Chloe shook her head.

"He isn't anything like Marc," TJ said in her defense.

"Nothing at all," her sister repeated sarcastically.

"What are you two arguing about?" Annabelle asked as she came into the living room with a plate of cookies. "Who wants milk?"

"Leave it for Santa," Chloe joked as she took a cookie. "We were arguing about men."

"So who's the right one for you?" Annabelle asked Chloe as she curled up in a chair and took a warm cookie.

"Justin," TJ said. "Is he still in town?" she asked Annabelle.

"Sorry, he moved away after he married some rich movie star." Annabelle almost choked on her cookie at her joke, before she said, "No, seriously, after Nici married, he was single for a long time. About five years ago, he married Margie Taylor and they moved to Bismarck, North Dakota, to farm her father's place. The marriage didn't last."

TJ raised a brow. "I'm amazed after being in town for such a short period of time how quickly you got caught up on all the local news."

Chloe groaned. "Excuse me, but we weren't talking about my lack of love life. We were talking about Silas Walker."

Her cell phone rang and she sprang to her feet. "Saved by the bell." She headed for her bedroom as she took the call from her agent.

"How are you doing?" Clara asked.

"Okay. I did the signing."

"I heard. Nice turnout?"

"Not bad."

"You made *The New York Times* Best Seller list," her agent said.

TJ knew she should be more excited about that. "That's wonderful."

"Not as high as last time, but it's early. Let's see if it stays where it is or goes even higher."

She was amazed how little any of this mattered right now.

"Have you heard from your True Fan?"

"A few letters, but I'm fine."

"Okay, but you don't sound fine. Maybe True Fan will give you a break over the holidays. When are you coming back?"

That was the question, wasn't it? "Not sure yet." She hadn't booked round-trip. Getting a flight could be difficult. But that didn't worry her either.

"Okay, I'll let you go. If you need anything…"

"I'll call. Have a wonderful holiday." She disconnected. She hadn't even asked where her book had hit on the *Times* list. Lower than last time. That was enough to know. She wasn't even tempted to check online. Normally, she watched closely the first few weeks of a release.

When she came back downstairs, Annabelle's fiancé Dawson Rogers was sitting in the living room. He got to his feet when he saw her, hugged her, wished her a Merry Christmas, then announced that he'd come to get them all for dinner out at the ranch.

"I decided to drive in for you since the visibility is poor and the roads are a little slick," he said.

She glanced out the window and realized he was downplaying how bad it was. "I hate to be a party pooper, as Grandma Frannie used to say, but I'm going to have to pass. Please give my best to your mother. I'm sure I'll see her over the holidays."

Her sisters started to put up an argument, but gave up quickly when they realized she had dug her feet in and wasn't going to change her mind. She wasn't in the mood for dinner and polite conversation. She had a terrible feeling about Silas that she couldn't shake.

As they all departed, she noticed that Annabelle had left the keys to her SUV on the hook by the door. She told herself that going out in this storm was more than risky. It might prove to be suicidal. Worse might be going to Silas's cabin when from what she could gather, there was a killer after him.

She thought about calling the sheriff. And telling her what? That Silas's former cop friends wanted to kill him? McCall couldn't do anything more than TJ could. That's when she knew that if she really wasn't going to do this, then she had not only to dress for the winter storm, but also to go armed.

"You're acting as if you think you really are Constance Ryan from one of your books," she said to herself as she went around the property getting things she thought she might need.

SILAS WORKED AS quickly as he could, given the weather. Another storm had blown in. Snow whirled around him, the cold wind biting at any exposed skin. When he'd first bought the land and begun to build on this spot, he'd thought about booby-trapping the area around it.

That was back when he'd been more worried about his former cops' plotting vengeance. He'd ditched the idea, fearful that he'd catch hikers or hunters in his traps and find himself in a lawsuit—if not worse. Also he hadn't wanted to live like that—fearing for his life every day.

Instead, he'd told himself that if they came for him, he'd deal with it then. As time went on, he'd begun to relax. Montana had that effect on him. He had liked feeling safe here, even knowing that it could change at any point.

Now as he finished loading the last booby trap, he stopped to listen. It was hard to hear anything over the wind whipping the pines and howling off the eaves of the cabin. He stared out into the storm, unable to see more than ten feet through the whirling snow.

Mad Dog would have the same problem.

Silas had worked hard since returning to the cabin. He'd known he didn't have much time. From the tracks around the cabin, he'd been able to surmise that Mad Dog had looked around, probably deciding how to come at him.

Now all he could do was wait. The question was where? Inside the cabin would make it too easy for his would-be killer. He couldn't depend on his booby traps stopping Mad Dog. All he could hope for is that one of them would delay the man long enough to give him the upper hand.

TJ STARTED THE SUV, then remembered something she'd forgotten in the house and, leaving the motor running, had run back inside.

Her heart was pounding. Common sense argued that she was doing a foolish thing. But that ache in her stomach, the feeling that Silas needed her, wouldn't let her turn back.

Inside the house, she found the flashlight she'd forgotten. It would be dark by the time she reached the cabin. She thought about texting Silas to tell him she was coming but he would just try to talk her out of it and right now she feared any reasonable argument would be all she needed to change her mind.

Back at the SUV, she was delighted to see that part of the windshield had cleared off. She used her gloved hand to take care of the rest. The snow was still falling so hard that it would cover it again if she didn't jump inside and use the wipers.

She climbed in, cranked up the heater even higher and turned on the wipers. To the steady clack, clack, clack, she shifted into Reverse and backed out.

It wasn't that far to the cabin. Once she was sure that Silas was all right… Text him, the voice in her head said. Text him. Don't make this drive in this kind of weather. Not to mention the fact that he wants you to stay away while he handles this.

She thought of Marc. She'd begged him to come home, but he was having too much fun. He loved the danger. He loved telling her about the close calls he'd had. She'd heard it in his voice. He thrived on the near misses.

Silas was different. He didn't want this. She remembered seeing both fear and dread on his face. *He knows he's mortal*, she thought. *He's strong, courageous, but only when it is demanded of him. He doesn't go looking for trouble.*

She was almost to the Zortman turnoff. She began to slow when she heard a sound in the seat behind her. Her gaze shot to the rearview mirror, her pulse taking off like a rocket as a face appeared a second before Tommy dove over the seat and dropped in beside her.

TJ screamed. The SUV swerved.

"Don't do anything stupid," he cried. "Keep driving or you're going to kill us both.

"Don't hit the brakes," he yelled as she hit the brakes.

The SUV went into another skid, but straightened as she jerked her foot from the pedal. Fortunately, there weren't any other vehicles on the road.

"What are you doing?" she demanded of him. "How long have you been back there?"

"I climbed in when you went back inside the house for your flashlight." He sounded so reasonable. "I couldn't leave things the way we did earlier."

"You were back there all this time and didn't say anything?" she demanded, furious with him.

"I wanted to see where you were going,"

Tommy said. "I had a pretty good idea. Nice to see that I was right."

"What do you want?"

He looked over at her in that irritatingly calm way he had about him. "Why would you drive up here in this storm? You're worried about him. You think he might have another woman in his cabin?"

"No!" She slammed her palm on the steering wheel. "I think he's in trouble. That's why you shouldn't have gotten into this vehicle. You're messing up everything."

"Wait a minute. You think this ex-cop is in trouble and you've come to save him?" Tommy reached down to look into the bag she'd brought. His gaze shifted to her at the sight of the makeshift weapons. He shook his head. "It's a good thing I came along."

"How do you figure that?" She didn't want him here, nor did she like him knowing the impulsive and no doubt foolish thing she'd done. Because seeing it through his eyes, she knew that's exactly what it had been.

The realization moved her to tears. She wiped angrily at them.

"What are you doing?" Tommy asked.

"Turning around and taking you back to town."

He stopped her with a hand on her arm. "I can help."

She looked over at him. Her skepticism must have showed.

"I have a little training for this sort of thing."

She continued to look at him.

"In the service. You do know that I was in the military, right?"

Did she know that?

"Just tell me one thing. Who wants him dead? The cops he put in prison?"

It surprised her that he knew so much about Silas. It made her wonder if his interest was before she came back to Whitehorse or if it was more about her.

"That's my guess. There's a man in town who wants him dead I'm afraid," she said.

Tommy nodded. "I wish I'd known that before we got here, but not to worry. Turn around and go into Zortman. I have a friend I can borrow a few real weapons from. Do you know how to shoot a gun?"

She shook her head as she turned around. That Tommy was taking this seriously made her feel less foolish about driving here, but just as ill-prepared.

Tommy told her where to turn once they drove into the tiny town. "Stop here." The moment she cut the engine, he grabbed the keys. "No offense," he said, and jumped out.

She waited, wondering what she'd gotten herself into. If Silas wasn't in trouble… Or even if he was, what would he think of her showing up with Tommy?

She didn't have long to consider that before he was back with two handguns and a rifle and who knew what other weapons he had under his coat. He tossed them into the SUV and then slid into the passenger side again.

"Let's go," Tommy said as he handed her the keys. "I know a back road."

She stared at him for a moment, realizing she'd never seen this Tommy, before she started the SUV.

Chapter Eighteen

Mad Dog came out of the trees and rushed the cabin like the wild man he was. He was almost to the door when he hit the first trip wire. The hatchet struck him in the thigh, falling short of the chest where it had originally been aimed.

The hit man let out a shriek of pain. The blade had left a nasty bleeding gash but did little to stop Kenny. He roared and charged the porch. The second booby trap sprung, this time working better than the first. Mad Dog was caught by his ankle and jerked off his feet.

He was hanging upside down from a tree limb five feet off the ground when Silas came around from the back of the cabin. He had only a second, not long enough to raise his rifle and shoot before Mad Dog fired.

The bullet grazed the size of his head. He rocked back, connecting with the corner of the cabin as he got off a shot. It went wild. He pumped another cartridge in and fired. Mad Dog howled with pain, swung around and let loose a barrage of bullets.

As Silas was diving behind the corner of the cabin, he caught another one; this one grazed his shoulder. He fired another three shots, all of them hitting their mark, but Mad Dog showed no sign that any of them had done mortal damage.

Silas's head wound was losing blood fast. He could see that Mad Dog was also bleeding, but not bleeding out fast enough. Mad Dog tossed a handgun away and pulled another. Even hanging upside down, the man didn't stop.

Silas ducked back as bullets pelted the corner of the cabin. He wiped at his temple and felt the darkness wanting to close in. He felt himself getting lightheaded. He had to finish this one way or another.

Firing around the edge of the cabin, he heard his bullets hit their mark but Mad Dog's only reaction was a roar of anger. Another barrage of bullets pelted the ground and the corner of the cabin as Silas ducked back again. Even upside down, Kenny was still a damned good shot.

He heard a loud crash and the splinter of wood and knew that Mad Dog had cut the rope he'd been dangling from and had crashed down on the bottom steps of the porch. He also knew that the man would be coming for him. There was a reason Kenny had been tagged Mad Dog Harrington.

With so many bullets pumped into the man, Kenny should be down for the count. But given the drugs he'd no doubt taken, Silas was wondering if he would be able to kill him before Mad Dog killed him.

Darkness faded in and out at the side of his vision. He blinked, trying to stay on his feet but feeling the effects of his blood loss. If he didn't finish this, and soon…

TOMMY INSTRUCTED TJ to kill the engine. "This is where we get out."

She looked into the storm raging around the vehicle and could see nothing but snow and the blur of the green pines beyond it.

"You might want to stay here," he said. "I'll come back and let you know what's happening."

TJ shook her head. She'd come this far. Now she had Tom involved in this. She had begun thinking of him as Tom—not Tommy anymore. He offered her a gun. She shook her head. "I'd probably shoot myself." Instead she grabbed one of her simple-to-operate weapons, ready to brave the storm and whatever else was waiting for them.

They exited the vehicle and Tom led the way through the woods as they dropped down the mountain. He motioned for her to be as quiet as possible. She could hear nothing but the wind high in the pines and the pounding of her heart as she tried to see through the snowstorm. All her instincts were still telling her that Silas needed help. But what if she was wrong? What if it was too late?

Snow whipped in her face and down her neck. She pulled her hat lower and coat tighter around her. They hadn't gone far when she spotted part of the cabin's roof through the trees. Tom motioned for her to stay back as he moved forward toward the back of the house.

They reached the outhouse. Tom stepped around it, TJ right behind him. She saw Silas first. He lay against the side of the cabin at its corner as if he'd just decided to sit down there. She couldn't tell if he was dead or alive, but the snow was red around him. She started to run to him, but Tom held her back.

A huge man came around the corner of the cabin holding a gun. He stopped to look down at Silas. As the man raised his weapon to finish the job he'd started, Tom lifted his rifle and fired. He kept firing as he charged forward until the big man returned fire.

Tom stumbled and went down. The big man limped over to him. She could see that the man was wounded and bleeding badly, but he was still on his feet—and still about to kill both men.

As the man raised his gun, TJ did something that even her heroine Constance wouldn't have done. She charged the man.

SILAS KNEW HE must have blacked out because when he came to, he was sitting in the snow.

Confused for a moment, he saw his rifle in the snow next to him and wasn't sure if it was still loaded or not. Snowflakes drifted around the corner of the cabin to melt on his face. He turned his head, not sure what he was seeing.

Mad Dog stood over someone lying in the snow a few yards from him. As the hit man raised his rifle to shoot the person, a figure came screaming out of the storm. With a jolt, Silas saw that it was TJ. She had a baseball bat in her hands.

Turning slowly as if not so steady on his feet, Mad Dog looked over at her as if he didn't believe what he was seeing. Silas felt the same way. She was so small compared to him. Mad Dog looked almost amused.

Silas tried to sit up, but felt his head swim again so he laid back. Just the act of pulling his handgun from his shoulder holster, almost made him black out again.

He finally managed to get it loose just as

TJ, still charging the man, swung the bat. The sound reminded him of a pumpkin left by kids in the street being crushed by a car tire. Blood shot out of Mad Dog's mouth and flew over the snow, leaving a bright red trail. Silas fired the handgun, emptying it into the crazed man.

For too many seconds, Mad Dog didn't move. Silas could see that TJ was ready to swing the bat again if need be. As Mad Dog started to lift his weapon in her direction, Silas yelled his name and tried to get up. The darkness closed in.

TJ SAW WHAT the big man planned to do. Silas sat bleeding by the corner of the cabin. Tom was down in the snow just feet away. She looked into the big man's eyes and knew she was about to die as he raised the gun in his hand and pulled the trigger.

There was a click, then another one, followed by two more, but no gunshot. The man looked

down at the gun in his hand, as confused as TJ
for a moment. Her heart pounded so hard her
chest ached. Her throat had gone dry. She'd
looked death in the face.

She swung the bat. It caught him completely
off guard. This time, his head snapped back as
the bat connected with his temple. He dropped
like a sack of potatoes. She stood there, the bat
ready to hit him again if need be, trembling so
hard she could hardly hold on to the weapon,
terrified that he would get up again.

But he lay in the snow, his eyes open and
blank, and after a few moments she dropped
the bat and fumbled out her phone. As she did,
she heard the sirens. How was that possible?
She rushed to Tom. He was still breathing.
Then she went to Silas. He too was breathing.
He smiled up at her, then closed his eyes and
dropped off into unconsciousness.

From behind her, she heard movement and
swung around. Tom was on his feet. "I called

the sheriff when I went in to get the guns," he said as he approached her. Then he smiled. "You really are Constance."

Chapter Nineteen

TJ had plenty of time to think about Tom's words as she waited at the hospital for word on him and Silas. She still couldn't believe what she'd done. She'd acted on instinct and it had almost gotten her killed. If the crazy big man hadn't run out of ammunition in his gun...

Her sisters spotted her and came running down the hall, only to be reprimanded by the head nurse. They pulled her into the waiting room, both talking at once. She held up her hand and realized it was still covered with blood.

Both of her sisters saw it, their eyes widen-ing. Chloe dropped into a chair. Annabelle just stood there, mouth open for a moment.

"It's kind of a long story," TJ said. She told them what Silas had told her about the police officers sending someone to kill him and how she'd had this bad feeling that he needed her, so she'd decided to drive up to his cabin.

Chloe looked at her as if she'd lost her mind.

"I had just turned onto the road to Zortman when Tom popped up from the back of the SUV. He'd been hiding there waiting to see where I was going."

"Tom?" Chloe repeated, having noticed that she was no longer calling him Tommy.

"He told me he had experience in the military and wasn't letting me go alone after I told him why I was determined to check on Silas." Her breath caught in her throat at the memory of the crazed big man standing over Silas about to kill him when Tom starting firing at him.

"If Tom hadn't been there, Silas would be dead. You can't believe this hit man. The EMTs said when they're high on all these drugs these kind of men are nearly impossible to kill. I don't know how many times the man had been shot…" Her voice broke. "Tom was shot. He's in surgery."

"What about you?" Chloe asked as she reached over and took TJ's trembling hands in hers. "The sheriff mentioned something about a baseball bat?"

TJ nodded. Looking back it was as if it had been Constance Ryan who'd leaped out of her books to swing that bat. "He would have killed us all but he'd run out of ammunition in his gun. He pointed it right at me. The look in his eyes…" She shuddered at the memory. "I watched him pull the trigger again and again, but there was only this loud *click, click, click.*"

"What did you do?" Annabelle asked, on the edge of her seat.

"I'd already hit him with the baseball bat once and it barely fazed him. But I swung it again and that time..." She shook her head. "That time he went down and he didn't get up. Tom had called the sheriff when he went into a friend's house in Zortman to get guns. I've never seen him like that."

"And Silas?" Chloe asked.

"He's going to make it. He's lost a lot of blood and has a concussion, but he's going to be fine, the doctor said. Now I'm just worried about Tom. If he hadn't come along with me..."

Her sisters got up to come over and hug her as the doctor appeared at the door to tell them that Tom Harwood had come out of surgery and was doing fine.

SILAS OPENED HIS EYES. The room seemed too white. Was he dead? He blinked and brought everything into focus. A hospital room. For a moment, he couldn't remember what had happened. He touched his head. Bandaged and hurting like hell. Something shifted on his bed. He looked down to see TJ. She'd pushed her chair over so she was right next to his bed. Then she'd apparently fallen asleep with her head on the edge of her mattress.

He stared down at her, enough of last night coming back to him to make him scared for her all over again. She'd been at the cabin carrying a baseball bat? Or had he only dreamt it? He touched his bandage again and this time TJ stirred awake.

She blinked at him and brushed some stray locks from her face. "You're awake. How are you?"

"Alive. I think I have you to thank for that."

"Actually, it was more Tom Harwood. I'm sure you'll hear all about it. Right now, the doctor said you just need to rest."

"There is something about a baseball bat," he said.

"Don't concern yourself with that right now," she said, avoiding his gaze.

He wanted to throttle her. "I should turn you over my knee…"

She shifted her gaze to him and smiled. "There's time for that when you get out of here."

He laughed, even though it hurt his head. "You saved my life. I owe you."

"We can discuss that too," she said, still smiling as she took his hand and brought it to her lips.

TJ COULDN'T REMEMBER the last time she'd decorated a Christmas tree. She'd done little to her apartment during the holidays. From the back of her closet she would pull out a small fake tree that was already decorated and plug it in.

She had found herself dreaming sometimes of Christmas back in Whitehorse. Sledding and snowball fights with the boys in the neighborhood, hot chocolate back in the kitchen with their grandmother before decorating her truly ugly fake tree.

Today though, their grandmother's house smelled of pine and gingersnap cookies. Annabelle couldn't seem to quit baking. Her sisters had dragged in the tree they'd cut up in the Little Rockies and they'd stood it up. Instantly, it was like being in the woods again. Being at Silas's cabin, TJ thought.

"Is this practice for marriage?" Chloe had wanted to know when they'd found Annabelle in the kitchen early that morning baking. The house smelled of ginger and cinnamon, and TJ breathed it in as if it was her last breath. Her apartment never smelled like this, not that she baked. In the city, it was too easy to run down and pick up anything you wanted to eat.

This morning, the three of them had sat around the kitchen table reminiscing about Christmases past. They'd eaten warm cookies and milk for breakfast, laughing about some of their Grandma Frannie memories before deciding it was time to tackle the tree.

TJ had been the first one up, long before Annabelle began baking. Even before the sun was up, she'd gone to the hospital to see how Tom was doing. He was sitting up and had more color than the first time she'd seen him right after surgery.

"How are you feeling?" she'd asked.

"Not bad." He'd smiled. "You were amazing."

She'd laughed. "I could say the same about you. You saved my life and Silas's."

He'd given her an embarrassed shrug.

"Thank you, Tom."

"Tom," he'd said and grinned. "Does this mean that Tommy is behind us?"

She'd nodded.

"I'd ask if you've fallen for this ex-cop, but it's clear you have. Does this mean you'll be staying in Whitehorse? I'd like it if we could be friends. Just friends."

"Truthfully, the future is a bit blurry right now. But we can definitely be friends."

Now, she stood back for a moment to look at the beautiful tree her sisters had found and cut down all on their own in the mountains. It was a fir and smelled wonderful. The branches were thick and already naturally decorated with tiny pinecones.

"I'm so glad you saved Grandmother's ornaments," TJ said as she dug in the last of three boxes that had been full. She held up a paper angel. "Remember this one?"

The whole morning had been like that. Each ornament had a memory for one of them. That's why it was taking so long for the tree to get decorated. All those trips down memory lane had derailed them multiple times.

At the sound of someone at the door, they all turned and then shared a troubled look.

"I'll get it," TJ said and hurried to the door, expecting to see Carol from the post office standing outside. But it wasn't Carol. "Silas? I thought you weren't being released until tomorrow."

"I talked the doctor into letting me out. I had to see you."

TJ ushered him inside. He was limping badly, he had a smaller bandage on his temple, but he was alive and smiling. Her sisters said hello, asked about his health and then discreetly left them alone.

"The sheriff filled me in on everything that happened," Silas said after she'd offered him a seat. He leaned toward her. "TJ, you could have been killed!" He shook his head. "What were you thinking?"

"That you were in trouble. The feeling was so strong I couldn't ignore it."

His gaze softened. "I don't know how to thank you and at the same time, never do anything like that again."

She smiled. "I can't promise that. If I feel like you need me…"

He rose and pulled her to her feet and into his arms. "I do need you. But what am I going to do with you?"

"I bet you'll think of something," she said and he kissed her, pulling her into him as if he needed to feel her body against his as much as she did.

"Go to the Christmas dance with me?"

She laughed. "I haven't danced in years."

"Me either. But I heard there will be mistletoe." He grinned.

"Are you sure you're up to dancing? You just got out of the hospital."

His grin broadened. "Oh, I'm up for a lot more than dancing."

Just then Annabelle came careening down the stairs to race into the kitchen. Smoke billowed up from the oven. "I forgot my last batch of cookies," she cried, making them both laugh.

Silas pulled TJ to him and kissed her, backing her up against the wall. His gaze locked with hers. Then something crashed in the kitchen and they heard footfalls on the stairs and moved apart, laughing as Chloe appeared.

TJ couldn't remember being so happy. She wanted to pinch herself. When Silas looked at her like he was right now, she almost forgot about True Fan.

THE OLD GYM was rocking with the sound of loud music and the roar of voices as the Christmas dance kicked off for the season. It was a huge yearly event. Some listen to the music and watch from the bleachers as others danced. It appeared that the whole town had turned out.

The old gym had been decorated with lots of sparkly lights. It reminded TJ for a moment of the only prom she'd attended, which made her grimace. Then Silas had put his arm around her, bringing her back to the wonderful, amazing present.

Chloe hadn't wanted to come. "You both have dates."

"You're going," Annabelle had told her. "I promise you'll have fun."

Chloe had made a face but had finally agreed to come at least for a little while. TJ had seen her talking to three cowboys they had gone to school with and later dancing.

As Silas pulled her out onto the dance floor, TJ put her head on his shoulder and closed her eyes. She loved the smell of him, fresh from the shower and yet so male. He pulled her closer as they swayed with the music. She felt so safe in his arms. But it was so much more than that. That feeling of being complete, being content, being happy filled her.

She never thought she'd ever experience this. She'd been such a loner all of her life. All she'd ever wanted was to write. That had been her driving force for so long. Silas made her want more. Opening her eyes, she looked around the room and felt such a sense of community. She'd forgotten what it felt like being part of a small town.

As the song ended, she was shoved hard against Silas. She turned to see Joyce stumbling away. It appeared she'd been drinking because she turned to sneer at TJ and kept going.

"You know her?" Silas asked.

"Went to school with her."

He chuckled. "What did you do to her?"

"That's just it. Nothing that I can recall.

Sometimes I think I get blamed for things I didn't do."

As they both watched Joyce weave unsteadily through the crowd and disappear out the door, TJ wondered if Joyce could be the one writing her the threatening letters. The woman seemed so angry, she could be True Fan.

"Can I get you a drink?" Silas asked as they stepped off the dance floor. She could tell his leg was bothering him and said as much. He denied it.

"Fine," she said. "But let's sit out a few dances."

He smiled at her, cupping her cheek, his gaze locking with hers. "After this is over, I was hoping to get you alone."

Her heart hammered in her chest. Heat rushed through her, colliding at her center to make her cheeks flush. Pulse pounding at the thought of being alone with him, all she could do was nod. She watched him walk away and could tell that he was trying not to limp. She headed over to where her sisters had gathered.

"Who was that I saw you dancing with?" she asked Chloe.

"Cooper Lawson."

"Justin's best friend from high school," Annabelle said.

"Don't read anything into it, all right?"

TJ laughed. "So you didn't ask him anything about Justin?" Chloe shot her a warning look, but TJ noticed that her sister looked happier than she'd been for some time.

"Where's Dawson?" she asked Annabelle.

"Drink line."

TJ looked in that direction but she didn't see Silas. "Oh, no, there's Mrs. Brown."

Annabelle looked toward the door where Ester had just come in and now stood brushing snow from her sleeve. "I heard she had a series of ministrokes and it's changed her personality."

"Maybe she isn't as grumpy as she used to be," Chloe said, and laughed.

"Or worse," Annabelle said.

"I just remember how upset she used to get with me in her advanced English class," Chloe said. "She would go to write something on the board and actually break the chalk in her fury. She once threw the chalk at me, missed, but almost hit Kirt, who was behind me. Later I saw her in the teachers' lounge crying. I know I was terrible. But she was always singling me out, especially when she knew I hadn't been paying attention."

"No wonder she is always glaring at *me*," TJ said with a groan. "I swear she's mad at me because she has me confused with the two of you. I was the good sister." She was distracted for a moment as she noticed Joyce standing by the entrance. The woman was looking right at her before she pushed out the door. The look gave her a shiver.

SILAS INSISTED ON a last dance since it was a slow one. "I like holding you," he said as he drew her to him. "The problem is that I don't like letting you go and the holiday will be over before we know it." He drew back to look at her. "I was wondering if you'd like to come up to the cabin for a few days after Christmas. I know you'll want to be with your sisters for the holiday—"

"I would love to."

He smiled and let out a breath as if he'd been holding it. "I might even decorate the cabin."

"There's no need. The cabin is perfect just like it is."

"You really do like it," he said, sounding a little surprised.

She frowned. "Of course. I have such good

memories…" Her voice trailed off. "I know it was only one night, but I felt as if—"

"As if we'd known each other a lot longer." His smile broadened. "I felt the same way. I've never had that happen before. Dates are always so—"

"Awkward, and you promise never to go through it again," she said with a laugh.

"Exactly." His blue eyes sparkled in the twinkling Christmas lights. "But with you, it was different. With you—"

"It was nice."

He nodded and leaned down to kiss her as the song ended. They stood on the dance floor as people began to leave. He kissed her again, then stepped back as if just then realizing the dance was over. "I'll get our coats," he said, his voice sounding rough with no doubt the same desire she was feeling.

Her legs felt a little wobbly as she made her way toward the bleachers where her sisters had gathered along with Dawson and some other friends. She heard them discussing going down to one of the local bars for a nightcap or two.

She'd almost reached them when someone grabbed her arm.

"Dear, would you mind walking me out to my car," Ester Brown said as she latched on to TJ's arm with shaking bony fingers. "I think I might have overdone it."

TJ looked toward the cloakroom and the huge line. It would be a while before Silas could get their coats. Ester apparently had never taken hers off.

"It's just right outside," Ester said, as if seeing her hesitation. "It won't take you a minute." She tugged on TJ's arm and the two of them headed for the door.

TJ shot a look over her shoulder at her sisters. She got Annabelle's attention and called, "Tell Silas I'll be right back."

"Silas," Ester said as they reached the side door. "Is he your beau now?"

Was he? She supposed so. At least until the holiday ended. "He's just a friend."

"Sure he is," the woman said under her breath. "My car's right over there." They walked through the freezing night air. Unlike Ester, who was all bundled up and in snow boots, TJ wore only a party dress and high heels.

As they stepped outside, TJ saw Joyce standing in the shadow of the building having a cigarette. She could feel her dark eyes on them as they crossed the parking lot.

"That woman doesn't like you," Ester said, following her gaze. She still had a bony-fingered grip on TJ's arm.

"I can't understand why."

Ester chuckled. "Maybe she's read one of your books."

TJ glanced over at her. Mrs. Brown had a

sense of humor? She was still chuckling as they crossed the parking lot.

Fortunately, Ester didn't seem to have the breath for walking—and talking. She'd thought her former teacher might want to bend her ear about her books, but that didn't seem to be the case. While in apparently good shape other than those minor strokes she'd had, Ester appeared to be winded by the time they reached her car.

"You know, I'm not really feeling up to driving," the elderly woman said. "I hate to impose, but would you mind, dear? My house is so close by. You're welcome to bring my car back."

"I can walk. It's no problem." She was already freezing, but she couldn't say no. Ester seemed to be breathing hard. What if she was about to have another stroke? TJ definitely didn't want her driving.

"You are such a dear," Ester said as TJ helped

her into the passenger side, then, taking the keys the woman handed her, climbed behind the wheel.

Ester's home was only three blocks from the old gym where the Christmas festivities had been held. Snow crystals hung in the air as she drove, the night clear and cold. All TJ could think about was getting Ester home and then returning to the old gym—and Silas. Right now, in his warm, strong arms was the only place she wanted to be.

She started to park the car in the driveway, but Mrs. Brown had already hit the garage door opener.

"I prefer to keep my car in the garage," she said as the door yawned open.

TJ pulled the car in and had barely stopped before Ester had the garage door closing behind them. She turned off the motor and started to turn to the elderly woman when she saw what Ester was holding. Her heart slammed against the walls of her ribs. "What?" The word came out on a surprised and suddenly scared breath.

"Not very succinct for a woman who makes her living writing," her former English teacher said as she waved the gun at her. Ester was still breathing hard, but she didn't look at all incapable of pulling the trigger.

"In case you're wondering, I know how to use this," the woman said. "I'm an excellent shot. Get out of the car. I don't want to shoot you in my garage, but I will if you don't do exactly as I say. It will be a first for you."

"Why are you doing this?" TJ cried.

"Because I can't let you write another one of those awful books," Ester said. "You had so much promise." She shook her head. "Parents over the years have chastised me for being too blunt." She huffed at that. "Honesty, that's what kids need. Good, old-fashioned honesty. That's what I've tried to give you. But did you listen? Of course not."

TJ stared at her as realization froze her in place. "You're True Fan."

"Not anymore," the elderly woman said. "I said I would be until the end. Well, this is the end. Now get out of the car and don't test me, Tessa Jane. If you had listened to me back when you were in my classes… Well, it's too late, isn't it. You won't be embarrassing me any further."

Ester pressed the barrel end of the gun into her back and shoved her toward the door into the house. They moved through the kitchen and into the living room. TJ's mind raced. What was Ester planning to do? She'd said that she couldn't let her write another book. Was she going to shoot her?

As they moved through the house, she looked for something she could use as a weapon. But she saw nothing that would allow her to spin around and disarm the woman before Ester shot her.

She tried to calm down, telling herself that her sisters would realize she hadn't come back. They would look for her. Silas had gone to get their coats. When he returned and they told him where she'd gone he would eventually come looking for her. If Annabelle remembered to tell him. She had to believe that he would find her—that someone would find her—as Ester jabbed her with the gun and pointed toward a door ahead.

TJ heard the word "basement" and knew that she had to do something. Surreptitiously she slipped off her bracelet. Silas had commented on it earlier. It was silver with tiny silver trees on it. She'd bought it the day before because it had reminded her of his place in the woods.

"Mrs. Brown, you can't do this," she said rather loudly to cover the sound of her dropping the bracelet next to one of the chairs in the living room. If the woman didn't find it before someone came looking for her, they might see it; they might know that she was here.

"I've already done it," Ester snapped and, reaching around her, opened the basement door.

All TJ could see was darkness. Before she could react, Ester shoved her. She fell forward, screaming as she tumbled downward.

Chapter Twenty

When Silas returned with their coats he looked around, but he didn't see TJ. Her sisters, though, were standing over by the bleachers. Most everyone had already cleared out. A few stragglers were standing around.

"We were just going uptown for an after-the-party drink," Annabelle announced when she saw him. "Do you and TJ want to come along?"

The last thing he wanted was a drink, and he was considering how to decline without hurting anyone's feelings when he asked, "Where is TJ?" He thought she might have gone to the women's room and looked in that direction.

"She just took our former English teacher out to her car," Chloe said. "It will give us a chance to talk."

He tried not to laugh as she drew him away from the others. He'd been expecting the third degree from TJ's older sister so he wasn't surprised. "I love TJ."

Chloe waved that off as if it wasn't important.

"I want to marry her. I was thinking of asking her on New Year's Eve," he said. "But I was worried that it's too early. I don't want to scare her off."

"You hardly know each other," Chloe said, sounding shocked.

"I know her. I knew her through her books before I met her."

She huffed at that. "You think she's Constance Ryan?" Chloe shook her head. "She's not. She's a prude. She's a chicken. She's—"

"She's braver than you know," he said, remembering the woman who'd saved his life. "She and Constance have a lot in common."

"She's been hurt by a dangerous man before."

He nodded. "She told me about Marc. I'm not him." He realized he was still holding their coats. He looked toward the door. "Shouldn't TJ be back by now?"

"Mrs. Brown is probably out there chastising her for some improper grammar she found in one of her books," Annabelle said, joining them. "Remember what a stickler the old bat was? All that stuff about participles and gerunds? It's a kick that Ester reads TJ's books. But then again, TJ was one of her best students. She should be proud that TJ has made a career as a writer."

Silas looked at Annabelle, hating the sudden

worry that had begun roiling in his stomach. "How long have they been gone?"

"Quite a while," Chloe said, now frowning. "We'd better go save TJ from her."

Silas pulled on his coat and, taking TJ's with him, said over his shoulder, "I'll check on her. You guys go on to the bar." He headed for the door, but stopped before going out. "What kind of car does Ester drive?"

"An older model. As big as a tank," Annabelle said. "Blue, I think."

Silas told himself TJ was fine, but all his instincts told him otherwise. He thought about the boxes of old discolored paper. Mrs. Taylor had said she'd sold one of the boxes to someone from the school. A teacher? A former teacher?

Once outside he looked around. A few people were coming and going. He didn't see a big blue car. He didn't see TJ or Ester Brown. Maybe TJ had decided to drive her home. He ran back inside, asked for directions to the woman's house and then ran to his truck.

He told himself that TJ could hold her own with an elderly woman. But his fear was that she wouldn't see it coming.

TJ GASPED AS a glass of cold water was thrown in her face. She didn't know how long she'd been knocked out. After the shock of the cold water, she became aware of the pain. She hurt all over. Worse, she found herself bound with tape on the floor. In the dim overhead bulb Ester had turned on, she could see that her ankles were bound, along with her hands. Her arms and one knee were scraped and bleeding, and her head ached.

She looked up into Ester's weathered face, still feeling as if this couldn't be happening. Her former teacher had pushed her down the basement stairs. It was a wonder the fall hadn't killed her, and yet Ester didn't seem to be in the least bit concerned. *Probably because she plans to kill me anyway.*

She looked around the basement, still feeling as if her brain was fuzzy. She spotted a small desk with the old manual typewriter sitting on it. Next to it was an open ream of the discolored paper. The rest of the box sat on the floor next to the desk. She thought as her mind seemed to be clearing that this was the teacher who'd said she bought it to give to the school.

Ester had been down here secretly writing the letters? But not just those, she saw. The trash can next to the desk was filled with wadded-up paper. Even from where she was tied up TJ could see what appeared to be a stack of typed pages on the other side of the typewriter. A book Ester was working on? Why write down here and not upstairs? Why keep it a secret?

She saw that Ester was fiddling with something over by the stairs. TJ began working at the tape binding her wrists behind her. It felt a little loose. If she could get her finger under the last loop…

Ester, she realized, had been wiping TJ's blood off the basement stairs railing. The thought made her stomach drop. How long did she plan to keep her in this basement? Or was she going to kill her and maybe bury her down here? Ester knew that surely she'd never get away with this.

Unfortunately, as the woman turned toward her, TJ saw something in her eyes that told her Ester wasn't worried about getting away with it.

"Did you know that I used to do some writing myself?" Ester asked conversationally as she pulled up a chair in front of her.

TJ stared at her, wondering if she was hallucinating all of this. "I didn't know," she managed to say, since it appeared Ester was waiting for a response.

"Of course you didn't. I was talented, but I needed to make a living." At the edge of the bitterness was pain and regret. TJ had heard it before from aspiring writers. "I dreamed of writing books and being famous like you." Her voice broke.

TJ didn't know what to say. "Now that you're retired—"

Ester shook her head, the gun in her hand still pointed at TJ's heart even though she was bound to the chair. "It's too late."

She decided now wasn't the time to point out that Ester could have written in her spare time as a teacher. The woman had never married or had more to look after than a cat. Maybe she could have found time to write.

But it was clear Ester wanted to blame someone for the fact that she'd never written the books that she'd dreamed would have brought her fame and fortune.

TJ felt badly for her because there'd been a

time when she'd had to work at an eight-to-five job. All she'd wanted to do was write. She remembered the frustration. She had the feeling that if she could just write full-time, she could get published. She could support herself on her writing.

It had been hard back then, but she'd gotten up early in the morning and written as much as she could before she had to go to work. Then she'd written late into the night. It hadn't been easy and what she'd written wasn't that great, but she wasn't the only writer who'd had to make a living as well as write starting out.

"That's why you're so angry with me," TJ said, realizing what this really was about. Tessa Jane had the audacity to become a writer while Ester felt she'd been kept from it by students like TJ and her sisters.

"I had talent," Ester said angrily. "I tried to share that talent as a teacher with students like you. But you never appreciated it. When I wrote you the letters, I knew you wouldn't take them seriously if they were from me. That's why I didn't sign them. I thought I could help you…" Her voice broke.

So instead of writing her own books, Ester had wanted to rewrite TJ's.

She didn't know what to say, but she knew she had to say something. Ester seemed confused, as if now that she'd taken TJ, she didn't seem to know what to do with her. Had she just wanted her to know the truth?

"Ester, I'm so glad you've finally told me that the letters were from you. I didn't realize that you were just trying to help me."

Ester stared at her. "How could you not realize it? I told you—"

"But how could I trust it not knowing who the advice was coming from?"

The older woman stared at her. "As if you would have listened even if you'd known. You were impossible in my class."

"I think that was my sister Chloe, or maybe Annabelle. Mrs. Brown—"

"You're just trying to confuse me. I need to think." Suddenly she seemed agitated. The hand holding the gun was shaking.

"You don't want to hurt me. You need to let me go. This is not the way you want to end your teaching career."

Ester huffed. "I didn't even get a gold watch. A luncheon and a pat on the head before I was replaced with a young teacher who doesn't know grammar and couldn't care less."

"I'm sorry," TJ said, not knowing what more there was to say. Ester felt as if her life hadn't mattered. TJs heart went out to her.

"Actually, I owe you so much. I learned a lot in your class. I wouldn't have been as success-ful as I've been without you."

Ester cocked her head at her as if trying to judge if she was just saying this.

She rushed on, all the time still working at

the tape around her wrists. "I loved the writing assignments you gave us," she said, trying to remember one of them that Ester might
also recall. High school had been so long ago
and yet for Ester it had been only months ago.
It was no wonder the students had all run together in Ester's mind—at least TJ and her
sisters.

She thought about what Annabelle had said
about Ester having a series of ministrokes.
That could account for some of this strange
behaviour as well, especially if Ester had had
them in the past six months.

"My favorite writing assignment was a character study. Do you remember that?"

"Of course I do," her former teacher snapped.
"I used it in all my classes."

"I wrote mine about the hall bully. You liked
it so much that you read it to all your classes.
It was the first time I realized that I might ac-

tually be a writer. That I might actually succeed at it."

Ester got a faraway look in her eyes for a moment. "Rick. That was the boy's name."

TJ nodded and felt a ray of hope even though Ester was still holding the gun steady and pointed at her heart.

"I do remember that," Ester said, and looked confused again. Her gaze met TJ's. "Tessa Jane Clementine. Yes, that was one of my best." She frowned. "Your sister wrote about a character on television." She shook her head and sighed.

"You gave me hope that day. All I ever wanted to do was write."

Ester nodded, tears in her eyes. "That's all I wanted too."

"So you need to let me go. This is just a misunderstanding."

Unfortunately, the woman shook her head again. "I can't do that."

ESTER BROWN'S HOUSE was only a few blocks away. The moment Silas pulled up in front of the small white home, he saw that there were no lights on inside. Also there was no blue car parked outside. But there was a garage to one side.

Is it possible they would have gone somewhere else? He couldn't even be sure that TJ was with the older woman. But both Annabelle and Chloe had seen her leave with Ester. He told himself that TJ was so accommodating that she might have taken her by the gas station to fill up the car for her. Or even the grocery store for milk and bread.

But his gut told him that wasn't the case. Fear gripped him as he climbed out of the truck and ran up to the garage. He peered in. A big blue boat of a car filled the small space. He ran up the front steps, rang the doorbell and then hammered with his fist before trying the door. Locked.

Where the hell were they?

He tried to calm down. But he knew that something was terribly wrong.

He saw a loose brick in the planter that ran the full length of the house and jumped down to retrieve it. Back up on the porch, he threw the brick through the small window next to the door. The glass shattered. He knocked the lethal-looking shards aside and reached in to unlock the door.

AT THE SOUND of breaking glass upstairs, Ester jumped, and for a moment TJ flinched, fearing that she would accidently pull the trigger. They both froze, listening. Someone was breaking into the house.

TJ opened her mouth to scream only to have a balled-up sock stuffed down her throat. She gagged and tried to spit it out, but Ester held it in place with a strip of tape.

"Stay here," she ordered before taking the gun and starting for the stairs.

Like she was going anywhere bound like this. But she had managed to loosen the tape on her wrists. She waited until Ester's back was turned as she headed up the stairs before she worked frantically at the tape. Whoever had come to rescue her wouldn't be expecting Ester to be armed. That could be a fatal mistake.

SILAS HAD JUST gotten the door open when Ester Brown appeared. She still wore her coat as if she hadn't been home long. Her hands were in the pockets. She didn't look that surprised to see him or that upset that he'd just broken into her house.

"What do you think you're doing?" she demanded in a voice that reminded him of a teacher he'd had in middle school.

"Where's TJ?"

"TJ?" she asked, and frowned as if the name didn't ring a bell.

"Tessa Jane. She helped you out to your car, possibly drove you home?"

Ester frowned. "Well, yes, but the last I saw her was in the parking lot with Joyce Mason."

He thought of the woman who'd seemed to purposely bump into TJ at the dance. He'd seen Joyce's expression. It had been hateful. For a moment, he thought he'd broken into the wrong house. But then he saw something over by one of the chairs and recognized it at once as the bracelet TJ had been wearing at the dance tonight.

Ester had followed his gaze—and seen it as well. She stepped to the side as if to block his view, but then must have realized it was too late. Her face filled with anger.

"Ester, what have you done with TJ? TJ!" he called.

"She can't hear you."

He started to rush past her when she pulled the gun. It looked so incongruous that for a moment he thought it was a joke.

But one look in her eyes and he knew this was no joke. His heart dropped at the thought of what she could have already done.

"As I told Tessa Jane, don't try me," she said. "I know how to use it. I don't want to shoot you, but I will." Her voice was so calm he froze. He wasn't quite close enough to her to disarm her. Nor did he doubt she would shoot him. Something in her eyes.

"Where is TJ?"

"You'll see soon enough," Ester said. "Close the door. You'll have to pay for that window you broke." She leveled the gun at him. "Unless you're dead too."

TJ HAD HEARD Silas calling for her. Fear gripped her for a moment as tears blurred her eyes. Ester had taken her gun when she'd gone upstairs. The woman didn't look like someone who would carry one—let alone use it.

And that could be Silas's fatal mistake. TJ had certainly underestimated the woman. She wouldn't make that mistake again, but Silas might not get a second chance. I might not either, she thought, her heart pounding.

She heard nothing from upstairs. No gunshot. Ester hadn't killed him. Yet. She waited a moment as if expecting to hear a gunshot and praying she wouldn't.

Then she went to work on the ropes on her wrists again. Now she worked even more frantically, feeling as if time was running out. As she worked, she listened. Earlier, she'd heard someone ring the doorbell numerous times and then the loud knock; she should have known it was Silas. Of course he would come looking for her. The sound of breaking glass had startled her as well as Ester.

What terrified her was that Ester seemed to

know that she would never get away with this. She didn't seem to care. It was as if this was something she'd decided to do before she died. Ester was determined to see this through even though it made little sense.

But TJ had seen the anger that had been apparent in the letters. Ester was furious with herself, with the world. And TJ had become the object of that anger.

The tape gave. She shoved it away, aware of the pain in her shoulder. Her arms were scraped and bleeding, her wrists aching from being taped up for so long behind her. But she barely noticed.

Tearing off the gag, she thought about calling to Silas to warn him, but realized that might put him in more jeopardy. But what if he believed Ester when she said that she wasn't here? What if he left?

Instead, she hurriedly untied her ankles and got to her feet, blood rushing into her extremities as she looked around for a weapon before she started up the stairs at a run.

SILAS COULD SEE that Ester seemed out of breath, but she still held the gun in her hand plenty steady enough to kill him. He'd complicated whatever plan she'd had and he knew it. But he could see the wheels in her head turning as she motioned for him to lead the way down the hallway.

"Where are we headed?" he asked, walking slowly. He could feel her behind him, intent on keeping that gun leveled at the middle of him.

"Don't worry about it," she snapped. "Just keep walking a little farther."

Ahead he could see a door on his left and an opening into the kitchen off to his right. The tension in the air was thick as salami. Ester was in planning mode and that was making him very nervous.

He was almost to the door on the left when

he heard footfalls. It dawned on him that someone was running upstairs from the basement
about the time the door was flung open. TJ
came bursting through it.

Silas only had a second to decide what to
do. He spun around, bringing up a foot. Ester
had been distracted for only a moment, but it
was long enough that she hadn't gotten a shot
off. He kicked at the gun in her hand, but the
woman must have had a death grip on it. All
he accomplished was shoving the gun off to
the side.

The report of the shot was deafening in the
small hallway. Sheetrock exploded on the wall
to the right, sending a cloud of chalky dust into
the air. Silas rushed Ester, but not before she
fired again. She was already swinging the gun
back in his and TJ's direction when it went off.

He grabbed the woman's arm, heard her cry
out as he wrenched it hard enough to take the
gun from her bony fingers. She attacked him

with her hands, flying at him. For her age, she was much stronger than he'd expected. With the gun still in his hand it was hard to wrestle her into compliance. He finally shoved her face-first into the wall and held her there as he pocketed the gun.

He realized he hadn't heard a sound out of TJ. Turning to look, at first all he saw was the open basement door. Past it was a bare foot, the high heel shoe she'd been wearing lying next to it.

"TJ?"

No answer.

He fought to move the struggling Ester along the wall so he could see TJ. Reaching the door, he slammed it closed. Sitting in the hallway staring was the woman he'd fallen in love with even before he'd met her. She had a hand over her side, blood leaking from between her fingers.

"TJ!" he cried, giving up on trying to hold

Ester. He opened the basement door and put her down on the first step before closing the door and locking it. Then he dropped beside TJ and tried to call 911 at the same time as he worked to stanch the bleeding. "You're going to be all right," he kept saying, praying it would be true. "You're going to be all right."

He held her as the sound of sirens filled the air.

Chapter Twenty-One

TJ remembered little after she was shot other than being in Silas's arms and then holding his hand in the ambulance. It had all seemed like a bad dream. Or an ending to one of her books. The scream of the sirens. The blood. The feeling that it was over and yet not knowing if everyone would get out alive.

She vaguely remembered seeing her sisters as she was being wheeled down to surgery. They were both crying. Chloe telling her not to die. Annabelle saying something about Christmas. And Silas standing at the end of the hall, his face a mask of pain and worry.

The rest was a blur of dreams and waking up in the middle of the night to see a nurse bending over her.

"It's all right," one nurse had said when TJ had been startled by her, making one of the machines go off. "You're safe here. It's all right."

She was in and out of consciousness so much that she hadn't known what was real and what wasn't. At one point there was a doctor standing over her. He was talking to someone. Silas. She'd felt his hand take hers and when she woke again it was still dark and she could hear Chloe arguing with the nurse outside her door.

Or maybe she'd dreamed it all. When she finally did surface in the daylight, TJ thought all of it had been a bad dream. But she was groggy from the drugs, lying in a hospital bed, so she knew that at least getting shot had been real.

Silas sat beside her bed—just as she had

sat beside his. He rose when he saw she was awake. "How are you?"

She tried to speak but her mouth was so dry. He poured her some water and helped her with the straw. The doctor came in then and told Silas he needed to check his patient.

"I'll be right outside in the hallway," Silas said, and left.

"You were lucky, young lady," the doctor said after checking her wound. "I was able to get the bullet out. No major organs were involved. It should heal nicely. Any questions?"

She shook her head because she had way too many questions. Some of her ordeal had come back, but the last part had happened so quickly...

The doctor hadn't been gone long when her sisters came in. She heard the nurse warn them that they couldn't stay long. One on each side of the bed, they looked at her with concern.

"I'm fine," she said, the words coming out in a hoarse whisper.

"That crazy old woman," Chloe said. "Who would have thought she was the one?"

"As mean as she was to me in English class?" Annabelle said. "I was scared of her."

"She was sick," TJ managed to say.

"Aren't they all," Chloe said. "She could have killed you. Almost did. If Silas…" She seemed to catch herself. "But you're safe here and it's all behind you."

"The doctor said you might be out before Christmas," Annabelle said. "But if you aren't, we're going to hold Christmas until you are."

"She doesn't care about Christmas right now," Chloe scolded their youngest sister. "Look at her. She's drugged up and probably in pain. Are you in pain?"

TJ was, but she shook her head anyway.

"If you're in pain, you just push this button," Annabelle said. "They told you that, right?"

Maybe they had. TJ couldn't remember. She struggled to keep her eyes open.

"Okay, that's long enough," a female nurse said from the doorway, and her sisters were shooed out.

TJ closed her eyes. A few moments later she heard the door to her room open and close softly. She knew who it was before he took her hand. She kept her eyes closed, feeling herself drawn back into the darkness. With her hand in his, she slept.

THE DOCTOR FINALLY insisted Silas go home and get some sleep. He knew he needed a shower, a shave and clean clothes. He also needed sleep. He hadn't had much since the dance.

But when he closed his eyes, he kept reliving the scene at Ester Brown's house. The sound of the gunfire, seeing that one bare foot and high heel shoe lying next to it. The scene was the kind nightmares were made of.

Even when he told himself that she was going to be all right, he still couldn't sleep. He'd never been so afraid. Even Mad Dog hadn't terrified him the way Ester had because he'd looked into her eyes and he'd known that she had nothing to lose. She would have killed them both that night. As it was, she'd almost killed TJ.

"So you don't know when you're coming back to the city?" Cal had said when he'd called him.

"No. Honestly, I'm not sure I am. Things are too up in the air right now."

"Are you worried that the cops you fingered will hire someone else to come after you?" his friend had asked.

"No, Kenny 'Mad Dog' Harrington did me a favor," Silas had said with a chuckle. "He taped their conversations, including when my former

NYPD partner paid him for his services. Mad Dog wasn't as stupid as they thought he was. He was worried that he'd take care of me and then they would turn on him to insure that he wouldn't rat them out some day when he got picked up for another crime. Mad Dog would have sold them out for a lesser sentence and they knew it. He was right. They would have had him killed to tie up the loose ends."

"Why haven't I heard about these tapes?" Cal asked.

"Could be because he made copies and made sure I had one. He left it for me in my cabin. I didn't see it until after he was dead. Apparently he wanted me to know who'd hired him before he killed me. So now, if they ever make a move on me, the tapes will surface."

"Tapes?"

"He made copies. Now the copies are being held in several safe places as…insurance. There's one on its way to you," Silas said. "My former…associates have been notified. They don't want any more years behind bars, or, in my ex-partner's case, he doesn't want to go straight to prison."

"So," Cal said. "This has to be about a woman."

Silas laughed. "Isn't it always? Only this woman, well, she's a keeper. That is if she'll have me."

THE NEXT TIME TJ WOKE, she found Sheriff McCall Crawford next to her bed. "The doctor said I could ask you some questions if you're up to it."

She nodded. "Ester?" The moment she saw McCall's expression she knew.

"Ester had another stroke," the sheriff said. "She didn't make it."

TJ felt a well of sadness. Yes, the woman had terrorized her and almost killed her, but she felt sorry for her too. "She felt she was never appreciated. She gave up her dream to be a teacher—at least that's the way she saw it."

The sheriff pulled out her notebook and recorder. "Why don't you tell me what happened."

She did, finishing with, "I don't remember all that much after I was shot."

McCall closed her notebook and shut off the recorder. "We found the typewriter and paper downstairs. She was definitely the person who'd been sending you the threatening letters."

TJ nodded. "There were other typewritten papers down there. Is there any chance I could have them?"

The sheriff hesitated. "It would be up to her relatives. I've been trying to find out if there are any. So far I've had no luck."

"What Ester wanted more than anything was to publish," TJ said. "I don't know if she even finished the book she was working on, but if there is any way it is publishable… I'd like to do that for her."

McCall smiled. "I'll make sure you get whatever there is."

Chapter Twenty-Two

TJ made it home for Christmas. She was still sore and had been forced to assure the doctor that she would take it easy. But Christmas Eve she was with family. Annabelle had always been like a kid in a candy store at Christmas. She'd baked and her future mother-in-law had brought over more food than they could eat in a month.

"Willie's teaching me to cook," Annabelle had said. "But we both think I have a way to go before I serve it to humans. The pigs out at the ranch love my cooking though," she added, making them laugh.

"Wait," TJ said as she remembered. "Belle, you were going to get married on Christmas!"

Her sister shook her head. "It just didn't work out. I couldn't get married without you there."

"I don't want to be the reason you didn't get married," she said. "I know how anxious you and Dawson are to tie the knot."

"It's not that big of a deal. We're thinking New Year's Day. It's just going to be a few people, nothing extravagant. Willie is insistent that it be held at the ranch and we let her take care of everything. I have the coolest mother-in-law-to-be ever." They agreed she did.

They ate, opened presents and sat around talking. TJ hated the months they'd been estranged and swore she was never going to let it happen again. "I wish Grandmother was here."

"Me too. I would love to ask her some questions," Annabelle said.

Chloe got up to adjust one of the ornaments on the tree. "It just goes to show that you never really know a person. Grandmother. Ester. Who knows what secrets everyone in this town has?"

"You're talking about how I make a living," TJ said. "If you assume everyone has a secret, well, it makes a good story."

"Have you read Ester's novel?" Chloe asked.

She nodded. "The sheriff said that no relatives have come forward. Once Ester's estate is settled, I'm going to self-publish it under her name."

"Is it any good?" Annabelle asked.

TJ hesitated, making Chloe laugh.

"You can tell us if it's awful," her sister said.

"After all, she tried to kill you," Annabelle added, and was quickly chastised by Chloe for bringing that up on Christmas Eve. "Come on, it's like the elephant in the room. If it hadn't been for Silas, TJ would be—"

"The book isn't very good, but it was Ester's first," TJ interrupted.

"And last," Chloe said.

She nodded. "I know it probably seems silly to publish it."

"No," Annabelle said. "It's sweet and more than the old bat deserves." She mugged a face at Chloe.

"So does this mean you're ready to go back to writing soon?" Chloe asked her.

"In a while."

Annabelle grinned. "She has other things on her mind."

"Speaking of Silas," Chloe said. "I hope the two of you are going to give it some time before you do anything rash."

TJ laughed. "Anything rash?"

"Leave her alone," Annabelle said. "Let her do whatever she wants to. It's her life and Silas is…"

"At the door," TJ said after there was a knock and he put his head in.

"I don't want to interrupt."

"You're not," Annabelle said, getting to her feet and motioning for Chloe to do the same. "We were just leaving." She ushered Chloe up the stairs, the two arguing all the way.

"I didn't mean to run them off," Silas said.

"It's fine. We just finished opening our presents. The two of them were starting to argue over me."

"Good thing I showed up, then," he said with a grin. "How are you?"

"Still sore, but the doctor said I am healing well."

"What about mentally? You've been through some traumatic holidays," he reminded her.

As if she needed to be reminded. "It hasn't been dull, that's for sure. But there won't be any more True Fan letters. There's no reason I can't get back to work. I have a deadline looming... What about you?"

Silas sat down across from her and took both of her hands in his. "Are you well enough that you still want to come up to the cabin with me?"

She smiled. "It's just what I need. *You're* just what I need. That and your homemade bread."

"You've got it. I'll pick you up tomorrow. Say, nine? Will your sisters be all right with it?"

"I don't need their permission."

"How about their blessing?" he asked. "I want them to like me because if I have my way…" He shrugged.

"I'll see you in the morning."

She went to the window and waved as he drove away, wondering if she would be able to sleep tonight. She was excited about returning to the cabin, but even more about spending the next few days with him up in the mountains away from everyone.

"You can come back down now," she called up the stairs to her sisters. She knew they hadn't gone far and had been listening to everything she and Silas had said. Annabelle because she was nosy. Chloe because she was worried.

They both came down the stairs, Annabelle all starry-eyed. "He wants us to like him because he's going to ask you to marry him," she said in a sing-song fashion.

"And live in that one-room cabin?" Chloe demanded.

TJ shook her head. "You're both way ahead of yourselves. Slow the roll," she said, something she hadn't said since high school. Both sisters laughed.

"Then why are your cheeks flushed?" Annabelle asked. "You're in love with him and he's crazy about you. Just make sure that you're back for my wedding on New Year's Day."

"I wouldn't miss it for anything," TJ said.

Chapter Twenty-Three

TJ almost didn't recognize Silas. He'd shaved off his beard and trimmed his hair. He no longer looked like a mountain man when he came to pick her up.

"Are you leaving?" she asked, thinking he'd done this because he had been called back to his job in New York City.

He shook his head. "I thought you might want to see what I really looked like."

She laughed, amazed that the man could be even more handsome without the full beard. She reached out and cupped his cheek, his strong jaw covered in designer stubble. "I'd take you either way."

He grinned as he stepped closer. "That's what I wanted to hear." He pulled her to him. "Ready to spend a few days at the cabin?"

TJ had never been more ready for anything. Silas drove through the snowy landscape toward the Little Rockies. It was one of those incredible winter days in Montana, not a cloud in a robin-egg blue sky, the sun making the new snow shine like fields of diamonds.

She felt herself relax. She'd come home to hide out from True Fan and make up with her sisters. Instead True Fan had been here waiting for her. The sheriff had told her that Ester used former students who'd moved away to mail the letters for her, including one now living in New York City.

"I suspect she was the one who took the photograph of your apartment," McCall had told her. "They just thought Ester was a fan."

She felt only sadness when she thought of Mrs. Brown. All those years when Ester was teaching, she had yearned to write, not realizing the only thing that had held her back was her own fear, her own misgivings about her talent.

"It is so heartbreaking," she'd said. "And yet what I told her was true. She helped me become a writer. She felt she'd wasted her life and it just wasn't true. I'm just sorry that I never thanked her for what she did do for me. Not until it was too late."

"But you got to tell her," McCall had said. "I'm thankful it ended without either of you being killed. The doctor said a lot of her behavior was due to the strokes she'd been having for some time. I don't think she realized what she was doing."

TJ looked out at the passing snowy foothills and reminded herself that it was over. She'd had a wonderful Christmas and felt closer to her sisters than she had in years. Glancing at Silas, she had to smile to herself. Annabelle was right. She was in love.

"I don't think I'm going back to New York," he said, and glanced over at her. "I don't need the job financially or emotionally or mentally. To tell you the truth I don't want to leave Montana."

She chuckled, as she'd been thinking the same thing since her return. "I love being here. And as you said, I can write anywhere. I was thinking earlier that I would let my New York apartment go. Chloe will be going back home to work and Annabelle will be getting married New Year's Day and moving in with Dawson, so the house will be empty. There's no reason I can't stay."

He grinned over at her. "I can't tell you how much I was hoping you would say that." He sounded relieved. "I want to spend as much time as I can at the cabin, but eventually either build a larger place or buy one."

"You wouldn't sell the cabin though, right?" she asked.

"No. Never. It's even more special to me since I got to share it with you."

As Silas pulled up in front of the cabin, she saw that the woodstove was going. Smoke curled up into the snow-filled pines. She couldn't wait to get inside, but he had other plans. As she started to open her pickup door, he stopped her.

"There's something I want to do first," he said, and reached into the pocket of his sheepskin coat to pull out a small jewelry box.

TJ felt her heart leap as she looked from it to his blue-eyed gaze.

"I know this is silly, but once we get into that cabin with that bed right at the center of the room, I'm going to want to make love to you. And maybe it's old-fashioned, but I want to do this right." He shifted in the seat and found a way even in the cab of the pickup to get down on one knee.

Sunlight poured through the window. Outside the fresh snow gleamed. In the warm cab of the pickup, Silas said, "Tessa Jane Clementine, will you marry me?"

She broke into a wide smile as tears filled her eyes. "Yes. Oh yes."

Silas slipped the ring on her finger. The pear-shaped diamond shone like the snow outside the windows. The ring fit perfectly.

TJ threw herself into his arms. The kiss was a promise of what was to come. Years cuddled up in that cabin. Late-night card games. Homemade baked bread. Best friends forever.

But for tonight, all TJ wanted was to spend it in this man's arms listening to the wind in the tall pines and the crackle of the fire in the woodstove. She was home.

SILAS FELT LIKE a man who'd won the lottery. He turned off the pickup engine, ran around and pulled TJ out and into his arms.

"I believe you're supposed to do this *after* we're married," she said, laughing as he carried her up the porch steps and over the threshold into the cabin.

"I feel as if our lives are starting now," he said as he put her down. He looked into her blue eyes. "Beautiful and smart and talented. How did I get so lucky?"

"You liked my books."

He laughed. "But nothing like I like their author." He kissed her, pulling her close. Outside, snow crystals danced in the air against the big sky. Inside, the woodstove crackled and popped invitingly. "How soon can we get married?"

She looked up at him in surprise. "As soon as we can find a preacher."

"I love you," he said, his gaze locked with

hers. "I think I left that out earlier. Also I forgot to ask you how you feel about kids."

"I'm for them," she said. "Two, three…"

"Four, five…" He laughed, still feeling as if he needed to pinch himself. "Tell me this isn't a dream."

"If it is, I don't want to wake up," she said. "I love you, Silas Walker. I know this happened fast. But I know it's right."

"I've never been this sure of anything." He kissed her, determined to find a preacher soon and make her his wife.

* * * * *

LET'S TALK
Romance

For exclusive extracts, competitions
and special offers, find us online:

 facebook.com/millsandboon

 @millsandboonuk

 @millsandboon

Or get in touch on 0844 844 1351*

For all the latest titles coming soon,
visit millsandboon.co.uk/nextmonth

*Calls cost 7p per minute plus your phone company's price per
minute access charge